ZOMBIE
DAY CARE

CRAIG HALLORAN

Zombie Day Care - Impact Series: Book 1
Copyright March 2014 by Craig Halloran

TWO-TEN BOOK PRESS
P.O. Box 4215, Charleston, WV 25364
www.twotenbookpress.com

Third Print Edition: 2014

ISBN Paperback: 978-1480-198456
ISBN Ebook: 978-0-9827799-2-7

Information about this author and his other works available at:
www.thedarkslayer.com

Publishers Note:
This book is a work of fiction. Names, characters, places, and incidents either are the product of the author's imagination or are used fictitiously, and any resemblance to the actual persons, living or dead, events, or locals is entirely coincidental.

CHAPTER 1

Location Unknown

H E WAS SHUFFLING OVER THE hillside with a look of desperation on his face. Sweat glistened over his crumpled brow and his curly brown locks were matted and coated with dirt. He looked over his shoulder, gasped and pushed forward. His elbows and knees were scraped and caked with dried blood. His jeans and shirt were in tatters. He clutched his sides as he jogged into the bright sun lowering over the horizon. He could make out the black silhouette of a small town miles ahead. *I can do it.*

He felt like he was in summer football practice, pushing himself to the limits, body quivering from exhaustion. This training was different. This time, if he stopped, he was dead. He didn't like football practice; he hated it...they all did. He remembered the smoking scowl of his least favorite coach shouting behind his back, 'Move it whale tail!'

He was a cumbersome teenager back then, stuck on the team's interior line, which was pure agony. He was good at standing in people's way, so he got the start. It didn't hurt that he was big either, except today being bigger was far from better. He would have done anything to be a little guy who could run like the wind. He ran the best he could, long heavy strides turning into a pathetic jog.

His big belly groaned with hunger and fear. He didn't know how far he had run. He remembered his last meal though. Yesterday morning. It was fast food, Taco Bell and Mountain Dew, eight dollars worth. His concern subsided for a moment, but a loud moan not so far behind him jolted his nerves. Fear gave his legs new strength. His feet ached and burned with each heavy step as he pushed on. He took a quick glance over his shoulder. Something was back there, trudging after him in the distance. He heard another moan.

The world had turned upside down. Zombies were real. They were taking over. It didn't all start in some small town, either. No, it was a meltdown in major cities. The outbreak spread like fire, New York to Beijing to Moscow. Zombies cropped up everywhere and flipped the world into turmoil. He, his friends and family headed for the hills. The hills were alive. They all fought hard after the surprise. He watched his loved ones get afflicted and devoured. They came for him, but he manned the higher ground. He blew their brains out, all of them except one. He ran out of ammo and made a dash for his car. He drove away until he ran out of gas, just a few miles from where he left.

He had dozed off, feeling safe and exhausted, in the middle of nowhere. He laid his head back just for a second, listening to the madness on the satellite radio. *America has fallen! Russia has fallen! The Middle East has fallen!* He fell asleep....

His eyes snapped open. A shuffle of dirt caught his ear. He wiped the drool from his mouth. The rear-view mirror showed nothing. His heart raced. Something was out there. A flicker of movement caught his eye in the side view mirror. He jerked out of the way just as a hand clutched for his neck. He scrambled through the passenger side door and fell outside.

The zombie was there, moaning at him. It came around the hood of the car. He moved the opposite way. *Now what?* It wasn't fast, but it just came steadily for him, like a stubborn child. He thought of Duck-Duck Goose. *Why did I think of that?* Around and around they went. He was uncertain what to do. *Just don't let it catch you.* His only option was to run into the town that was miles away. Maybe more zombies waited there, anywhere, everywhere...there was no choice.

He slipped around to the driver's side of his car, reached in the window, and popped his trunk. He was faster than the zombie, that much was certain. He couldn't run forever though. As it pursued him around the car he circled back to the trunk and reached in. He fumbled around, eyes never leaving the creature. He found a handle and pulled it forth. A small sense of security filled his body as he wielded a big wooden softball bat. It was a gift he bought for his girlfriend.

"This is messed up," he muttered.

He stepped around the car again and bashed in the back passenger window. Still the zombie came, quicker than before it seemed. He made another round to the smashed window, reached inside, cutting his arm on the jagged glass. *Idiot!* The zombie came faster now. He grabbed his backpack as his blood dripped down his arm. *Screw it!* He slung the pack over his shoulder. He hoped everything was in there. *Be prepared.*

He squeezed the handle in both hands. *I gotta do this now!* The zombie came on as he back pedaled away.

"Please don't make me do this. Just go away!" he said, waving the big bat.

Still it came, moaning. He looked at the bloody gash on its shoulder. A man-sized bite of flesh was gone as well as part of its dangling arm. The rest of the zombie was perfect. It was tall, full figured, and dressed in a pro-football jersey and tight jean shorts. He blinked hard. He could see the painted nails that once scratched his back and belly. Black was her color. Now she came for him, unsteady, black-eyed and slack jawed. Blue veins rose along her once soft and sensual skin. He couldn't believe he had to bash in the brains...of his girlfriend.

"No!" he screamed, hoisting the bat high in the air.

Still she came. He swore he could see a smile on her crossed mouth. Jeanine always had a smirk. He blinked hard again. It was something he always remembered. Deep down inside he still loved her, or it. He was ready to propose, but the world began to end. Still she came, chin down, shuffling his way. He wanted to hug her. His instincts screamed to kill her. Everyone else he knew was dead. He couldn't do it. He felt a lump in his throat rise as he let out a sob. *I can't.* He screamed, snatched up his backpack and ran.

He had been running ever since. Night was coming and the tiny town was getting closer. He tried to remember Jeanine the way she used to be, but could not. He was huffing along, fighting for breath as he tried to reach the town. He gave another look back and there she came, step after determined step. He could swear she was getting faster. She used to be faster than him anyway. He never minded running behind her before, but now he had to stay ahead to stay alive. It was a discomforting memory for Nate McDaniel.

CHAPTER 2

NATE WAS WALKING AS FAST as he could, often looking back over his shoulder. His zombie girlfriend was nowhere to be seen. The sun was dipping into the dusk as he made his way into the town. Pear trees and flower beds were planted along the streets. There were no stop lights, just signs and well-defined crosswalks. The polluted sounds of human interaction were vacant. He followed the railroad tracks across a rusting iron bridge as a wide stream of water flowed underneath. He was cautious. Zombies could be anywhere. He hoped there were none.

He cupped his hands to his mouth, but then lowered them. Maybe yelling wasn't such a good idea. Nate didn't want to alert the unknown. He knew better. He was starving now and his stomach hadn't stopped growling for miles. He was exhausted. He never remembered being so tired. His feet were aching and burning like fire. He had to find food. There had to be something left in this town. As he finished crossing the bridge, he looked back again. Nothing was there. He saw a black bird perched on a power line above, then something snapped and he lurched forward.

"Damn!" he shouted.

Blinding pain shot over his shin and up through his knee. His leg was wedged between two rotted railroad ties. His jeans and skin were torn just below the kneecap. He was bleeding and held fast. He tried pulling his hurt knee up.

"Ugh!"

It didn't help that he was over two-hundred and fifty pounds. He was dead weight, and the effort jammed his leg further down.

"No—No—No! Lord no!"

He closed his eyes and took a breath. The lowering sun went dark as a cloud passed. He felt the shade on his face. Somewhere a crow squawked and flapped away. He opened his eyes and looked back. He watched the black bird dart over the head of a figure. It was her. *Already!* She was coming his way. His chin dipped into his chest.

"Come on Jeanine!" he yelled, knocking his bat into the bridge.

His heart was sinking. He was stuck and she was going to eat him. His stomach coiled into a knot. His will to survive was not the strongest, but his desire not to be eaten alive was something else. Deep inside, fear consumed him. He pushed on the rotting boards. They groaned under the desperate power of his supple muscles. He strained in agony as she approached step by step, stumbling over the rotting ties.

Fall! Fall off the bridge dammit!

She came on, unfettered by her missteps, crossing the bridge only a dozen paces away.

How does she move so fast?

Nate couldn't comprehend how the slow-going figure stayed at his heels like a bloodhound. He thought of the story of the tortoise and the hare. He used to love that story.

He ripped his leg free with a scream. A torn slab of flesh and jeans was hanging down his leg. Thick splinters were burning deep under his skin. He saw muscle, or was it? *Don't look, idiot!* Tears watered down his paunchy face as he struggled to his feet. He saw a necklace hanging from her neck. He bought her that on her birthday...a gold crucifix. *Why couldn't she be a vampire?* She was almost to him. He ran on in a desperate limp despite the pain building inside his leg.

He needed a car, a truck, anything with wheels. *A bike!* He was parched. His body was already pushed beyond his limits. All of those tennis lessons never prepared him for this.

Had anything? He looked down at his knee. His blue jeans were soaked. A dark patch of material was sticking to his leg, and his shoe was bloody. His body became weak at the sight of all the blood. It's why medical school was never an option.

The sign of a small convenience store was in the distance. He forced himself forward. It seemed to take forever. He looked back and she wasn't there. He kept moving, holding his stomach because he felt so sick. He made it to the glass doors and tugged on the handle. It was locked.

"No!" he cried.

He pulled again and again, looking for someone inside. The shelves were half full, but there were no signs of people. Wiping the burning sweat from his eyes, he surveyed the parking lot and leaned back on the door.

"What the — !"

He fell inside the doors with a thud. As he looked up in bewilderment he noticed the words on the door: PUSH and PULL. A smile crossed his haggard face. He shoved the door closed and looked for a latch.

"Come on," he mumbled, "Come on!"

It was a key only lock. He screamed again. He hustled over to the register and rummaged his blood stained fingers through the shelves. He checked the counter. *Nothing!*

He pounded on the counter as he shouted, "Damn! Damn! Damn!"

He knew she would arrive at any second. What now? He tried something new.

Whack! Whack! Whack! He busted open the register with the bat.

He jerked open the drawer and found a key in one of the change bins. He snatched it and limped over to the door. There she was, passing the gas pumps. *Almost here!* He stuck the key in the lock, but it didn't fit. The key slipped through his fingers and clattered on the floor tiles.

"Shit!"

He grabbed the key and tried sticking it back in the keyhole. It didn't fit. *No!* He turned the key over and it slipped inside. Something slammed into the door. She was pushing from the other side of the glass, moaning at him. He shoved back, wedging his foot against a store shelf. He turned the lock, but the door was no longer shut. She was pushing him back inside. She was stronger than a man.

"No!" he screamed. He lowered his shoulder and knocked the door hard, shuffling her backwards.

Clatch!

He got it. "Thank God!"

He slunk down on the glass doors with a gasp of relief. He couldn't move. His leg was throbbing and he didn't have the strength to stand. His breathing was loud and he could feel sweat dripping off of his nose as he closed his eyes.

Wham!

Her fist busted into the glass, leaving a spider web mark. He rolled away, eyes wide. How much energy did he have left?

I can't do this.

"Go away!" he screamed. "Go away!"

CHAPTER 3

NATE TORE HIS JEANS OFF just below the knee. The bloody gash made him sick, and he spit up bile. He rummaged through the shelves and found some gauze, antiseptic, and medical tape. He closed his eyes as he placed the loose flap of skin back over his shin and knee. His eyes watered as he sprayed on the antiseptic. He pounded at the floor, biting his lip. He wrapped it with gauze and taped it off. He peered at the door as Jeanine pounded and moaned on the other side of the glass. The whole building seemed to shake with every blow.

He found an ace bandage, and his bloody hands wrapped it around his knee. The blood no longer soaked his bandages, but he still felt ill. He ripped off the top of a bottle of ibuprofen and limped over to the glass cooler doors. He found a twenty ounce bottle of Mountain Dew and pulled it out. He twisted off the yellow cap and read the inside.

"Better luck next time," he read, as he flicked it away.

He took a handful of pills and washed them down with the green liquid. It was luke-warm, but he still sucked the entire bottle down like ice water. It was delicious all the same and his stomach churned again. *I'd do anything for a burrito.* He tore into a box of snack cakes, washing them down with another bottle of the soft drink. He looked over at Jeanine, wiping his mouth on his sleeve, watching her continue to claw at the door. *I have to be dreaming. I can't believe I was gonna marry that.*

The sky was turning black as the sun dipped and a blanket of gray clouds began to roll in. He heard the soothing sound of raindrops landing on the metal roof above.

"Now it starts to rain," he said, as he sat down in front of the fountain drink machines across from the entrance door.

He sipped on his bottle, watching her hands bang and scratch at the doors. Her breasts jiggled underneath the black and gold jersey, and he thought of all those blissful mornings with her. *I'm sick. She's getting ready to eat me and I can only think about her tits.* Her face was a maul of horror. Her hair seemed to be drying out. Blue veins began to swell under her tanned skin. Nate wanted to pinch himself, but the effort wasn't in him.

Nate closed his eyes and tried to remember

Jeanine from back when. They had been together for years and she wasn't something he deserved. She had been a good person, but he had been bad. Not bad in the good sense, but rather bad in the pathetic, character lacking, "me first" sense. He was spoiled and brainy, a bit of a slob who ate too much, played video games, collected comics, and watched too many movies. *What a winner.* But he also had a golden tongue that tickled a woman's ear with all those words they liked to hear: I want you. I need you. I love you. They never meant a thing to him, until he met her. Jeanine was different.

She liked him for her own reasons, ones he never understood. They only had a few things in common; one of them was softball. He had the big bat and she liked it. They both were competitive and smart...maybe she liked that, he thought. He had the brains that got you a full scholarship anywhere, and missing classes still got him straight A's. It was the only thing he was better at than Jeanine. *That and video games.* Whatever the connection was they had, it was special, and he loved her every single day. Now she was gone, her haggard face etched forever in his nightmares.

Nate peered around the convenience store. Where was everyone? Many afflicted cities such as his fled the zombies who pursued them, that much he knew. He didn't see any dead bodies though. Whoever owned the store picked up and ran, hoping to return one day. He pulled the bat along his side and took off his backpack. Unzipping it, he reached inside. He pulled out his phone charger. He patted his pants pocket. His phone was still there. He squeezed it out and turned it on.

The display showed thirty percent battery life and no signal bars.

"Great," he said under his breath. He moved it around in the air and a small green bar appeared. He dialed 9–1–1. It was busy. He waited, and Jeanine's raps on the door were in a steady cadence now. Her moans continued, like a dying hound, and the glass and metal doors shook over and over. He covered his ears. *She never moaned that much with me.* He dialed again. Busy. He tried again. Busy — Busy — Busy. He fought the urge to sling the phone down, sighing aloud.

He stared at her long and hard. He had no choice. He had to kill her. He studied the softball bat he bought for her. It seemed like a crude way to go. He noticed the lighter fluid stacked by some bags of charcoal near the door. *Maybe I should set her on fire.* The smell would be disgusting, and there had to be a more humane way to kill her. It was the bat or nothing. At least he could bury her body then.

As darkness fell and the heavier rains

came, his taut body softened. The loud rain began to drown out her moans. It relieved him. He took another sip as his eyes fell closed. He was fast asleep as she still pounded away.

CHAPTER 4

NATE GASPED. A VIOLENT SHAKE awoke him from his deep slumber. His skin was cold and clammy. Sunlight from the storefront windows bathed his face and body. He rubbed his blurry eyes as his heart thundered in his chest. The double glass doors were still intact. Jeanine was still there, too.

Her head was now sticking through the glass and her jaw clutched opened and closed. It made him think of a glass stockade, but crueler. The only thing keeping her from pushing through were the tiny wires holding the safety glass intact. Nate grimaced as he could see the glass cutting into her neck. She made no effort to force her way back out, only forward. She was stuck, but the moaning continued.

"I can't take it anymore!" he yelled.

He got up growling. He noticed his leg was swollen and purple from the knee down. He grabbed a plastic bottle of Mountain Dew and limped over to face her. As he came closer, her mouth snapped open and closed like a cow chewing its cud.

"Sorry baby, I know you hate this stuff," he said, shoving the bottle, cap first, into her mouth.

If Jeanine had a flaw, it was talking too much. He fantasized about doing that many times before. She hissed in and out of her nose, as her wide mouth was filled with the green bottle over half way in. He stepped back, eyes looking about. An eerie sensation of peace fell over him. The moaning was gone.

She crunched down on the bottle that was stuck in her mouth. Green carbonation squirted into the air. Shaking her head back and forth, the bottle remained. He limped over and grabbed the bat.

This is it. Got to do it!

He looked into her dark, long-lashed eyes and knew nobody was home. There was no other way. It was her or him. *Until death do us part.*

As he approached, he could see her perfect white teeth biting deep into the bottle. It pinched inward and her eyes widened as she sucked on the bottle.

"What the hell?"

She seemed to be drinking it. Green fluid dripped down her chin and gashed neck. He could hear a wheezing and sucking sound coming from her. The bottle began to empty and started to collapse as if it were squeezed by a hand. The bottle fell and rattled on the tiled floor. He looked at her, the bottle, then back at her. He approached with the bat raised high. Her listless face was silent. He watched as she struggled to pull her head free, her eyes catching his, passing him over like he wasn't there. The hunger and aggression were gone. She was just stuck inside the glass, trapped like an animal, not knowing what to do.

"Now what?" he said, setting down the bat.

He waited minute after minute. The store was becoming hotter as the sun rose further. It was past noon and it must have been a hundred degrees inside. There wasn't a window to open. He had to pee and he headed for a bathroom in the back. His ears and mind were monitoring any signs of danger.

"Ah!" he said as he began to pee.

It was the most relief he had felt in forever. He walked back out and there she was, moving very little, a defeated creature. He felt bad for her all of a sudden. Did the soft drink cure her? What was going on? He took over another bottle and twisted off the lid. Her black eyes glimmered up at him. Her arms pressed the glass from the other side as the jagged edges had her neck still caught. Nate poured some to her lips. She didn't try to bite, but licked her lips with her blackening tongue. He noticed the liquid running down through a hole in her neck.

"Ugh!" he said, stepping away and spitting.

Her eyes were fixed on the bottle now. He had to get out of there though, as the sweltering heat was too much. The key was still in the lock. He crouched down and slid over to it. He reached up, unlocked it, and slid back away. She pushed the door in and she pulled it back out. It was in slow motion as she went in and out, back and forth, legs shuffling over the sweep. It reminded him of a cartoon and a revolving door. He stuffed some pop bottles in his backpack, along with some candy, nuts and protein bars.

Here we go. He mustered his courage and as she backed out again he shoved himself past her. He was free. *Yes!* He hid behind the gas pumps and waited. She kept moving back and forth. He checked his smart phone. One green bar showed with twenty percent battery power remaining. *Just get a car and go!*

He walked around the building. No cars. There wasn't a single one to be seen. He saw the backyards of tiny houses nearby with sheds on many lawns. *There has to be a bike in there.* He limped into one fenced yard. It had a decent-sized storage barn in the back. He straddled the rail and he fell onto the other side.

"Ow!"

The barn was padlocked. He knocked the lock off after several swings with the bat. He jerked open the doors and a pair of Schwinn mountain bikes hung in the back.

"Yes!" he said, pumping his fist. "Thank you Jesus!"

He lifted one bike down and got on. The pedaling was excruciating as he wobbled at first, but he was fine, he was moving. Taking the road, he rounded back in front of the convenience store. Jeanine wasn't there.

"Shit!"

He tried turning his head every direction at once, but she was gone. Fear filled him from head to toe as he listened for her. Nothing but the wind was with him, and very little of that.

He pushed off and pedaled around the store three times. He looked up and down the roads. All he saw were small houses and buildings, lined up side-by-side, with overgrowing lawns. Something crept up through his spine as he stopped back in front of the store. A large chunk of broken glass was crumpled on the ground. His heart jumped as he heard rustling coming from the inside, and that's when he saw her. She was wandering the aisles and knocking things onto the floor.

"Jeanine!" he yelled. No response.

He backed away, still straddling the bike. *Now what?* He got off the bike and walked inside. He poured more soda into a large cup and set it on the ground. She lumbered towards the cup and kicked it over, spilling the contents onto the floor. She kneeled to the ground and licked it up like a dog, every bit, giving Nate a disturbing feeling. *I can't believe this.* He wanted to cry. She grabbed the cup and tried to eat it. Nate had a crazy idea.

He poured a path of the soda along the floor and outside. He set the bottle at the end of the path. She lapped it up as she crawled on her hands and knees. He took out his smart phone and recorded her.

He held the phone high in the air. He got two green signal bars. He uploaded the file on You Tube reading: "ZOMBIES LIKE MOUNTAIN DEW! MUST WATCH!"

He posted a tweet: "MOUNTAIN DEW WILL STOP THE ZOMBIES!"

His smart phone died.

CHAPTER 5

A DOG WAS BARKING SOMEWHERE, FOLLOWED by more barks and howls. Nate hadn't heard them before. Now they seemed to come from everywhere. Even cats were darting across the abandoned streets.

He left Jeanine behind at the store. As he pedaled around the small town he noticed a Sheriff's detachment and came to a stop. He dismounted the mountain bike and limped to the door. It was open.

"Hello?" he said, waiting. He clutched his bat as he stepped inside.

It was a small red brick building with a teller window inside. *This is where they pay taxes and fines I bet.* A small waiting room was enclosed with three hard plastic chairs illuminated by glass-block windows. Another heavy duty door waited before him.

He pressed his ear to the steel door and closed his eyes. He heard nothing. He turned the knob, but it was locked. He kicked at the door, but it didn't give in. It just made his leg hurt even more. He grabbed one of the chairs and tossed it through the teller window with a loud crash, shattering glass all over the floor.

He sat up on the counter, careful of the glass, and slid to the other side. There were a couple of offices in the back that he searched around. He looked in a small break room with a table, chair, fridge and coffee pot. He checked the phone on one of the desks. There was a dial tone. He called 9-1-1. It was busy again. He slammed the handset to the ground saying, "Damn!"

He headed down a dimly lit hallway. There was a pair of small holding cells big enough for a few people. Handcuffs and keys were hanging from the wall. He clenched his fists and shook them. *This is good.* The shotgun rack was empty. *That's bad.* He stepped inside the jail cell and pulled a soda from his backpack. He twisted off the cap, sitting down on a metal cot anchored to the wall, and took a long drink. He took another swallow, set the bottle down and closed his eyes. He thought about his next step. Maybe he could find power in the town somewhere. He froze with fear as he heard the sound of scraping glass.

His heart was racing on the inside. Someone or something must have heard him break the glass door. He exited the small cell with his bat gripped in two white-knuckled hands. Something was following him. The sound of the crunching glass ate at his soul. Was it another zombie? Would he dare to peer through the small square window in the door he tried to kick in earlier? He wiped the sweat from his eyebrows. *Here goes.*

He peaked and screamed, "Gah!" He dropped his bat and clutched his chest.

It was Jeanine's face pressed into the window. *How did she get here so fast!?* He heard more scraping of glass as she dragged herself over the counter. He couldn't move. He looked down at the bat. *Grab it, idiot!* It seemed like he was in slow motion as he picked it up and began to back pedal deeper into the corridor. He felt the cold cinder block wall on his back...a dead end. *Sonuvabitch!* Only one other cell remained. He heard her coming, and saw her long gashed leg cross into the light. Her head poked around the corner followed by the rest of her full body. She slowly came his way.

"No Jeanine! Please stop!" he cried, stepping inside the barred door.

He began to pull the door inward the further she came. He felt like a coward now. He had a weapon, but he couldn't use it. Not on her. And what would happen if he didn't kill her...she would eat him.

"I won't be eaten! I won't be eaten!"

She was passing the first cell and he could hear her say, "Num-Num. Num-Num."

He could not make out her drooping face. She was a creepy silhouette of a woman with a dipping shoulder and a dangling arm. For someone that moved so slowly things seemed to be happening awfully fast. Nate realized he hadn't grabbed the keys. If he locked himself in the holding cell he would starve. He could see the keys hanging on the wall at the beginning of the corridor. *Idiot!* Now Nate wasn't sure which fate would be worse, being eaten or starving to death. *Why me?*

He shouted at the top of his lungs.

"Why me!"

Jeanine shuffled closer his way as Nate pulled the barred door further inward. Jeanine stopped, turned and entered the other cell. He stood transfixed as she looked through him. *Huh?* The light from the small window in the back of the jail cell displayed the scene as she reached over for his soda bottle sitting on the cot. He couldn't feel his legs as he watched her pick it up. *Shut the door, idiot!*

He didn't remember what happened next; fear and adrenaline wiped out his thoughts. Something slammed shut with a loud bang. He had her trapped inside. She didn't seem to notice a thing.

"Num-Num...."

CHAPTER 6

THE OTHER SIDE OF THE phone line rang again and again. If it wasn't ringing, it was a busy signal. Everything in the town was dead except for the phone lines. Nate sat in a recliner, propping up his aching leg. A dead television screen sat before him. A breeze billowed through the sheer curtains in the small home he occupied near the jail. Days had passed since he had locked Jeanine in the cell. He wanted to leave the town, but couldn't. He was too scared, and his leg wasn't getting better.

He loosened the bandages around his knee. *That's bad.* The gash was infected, swelling his leg. His gout had flared up, making things worse. His bare foot was fat like a pillow. He shut the recliner, grimacing at the jolt, and slipped on a red flip-flop he had taken from the convenience store. He grunted as he stood. Using the bat as a cane, he hobbled over to the front door, opening it into the rising morning sun.

The sounds of birds chirping filled the air. "Huh."

No dogs lay at the door. The bowl of food he set out was empty.

"Time to feed my girlfriend, I guess," he said, hobbling back down the street.

The bat echoed off the concrete sidewalk as he went. He had never felt so alone and trapped. Things were perfect a few months ago. There was a good job waiting for him once he finished his master's. He had a fine looking wife lined up, too. Now she was a zombie, along with the rest of the world. He wondered if he was the last man on earth and if he'd ever have Taco Bell again.

He had patched his leg up the best that he could, but the pain was a constant reminder that his purgatory wasn't over yet. *What did I do to deserve this?* He didn't have it in him to search for more medicine, and the town pharmacy was bare. Despair addled his brain as horrors lived in his sleep. He searched for a vehicle, but all he had was a bike. He couldn't bend his leg now, and he could barely stand the pain. His entire purpose was to feed Jeanine her Mountain Dew and hope somebody from the living swung by on a golden chariot. Anything would do.

The sheriff's depot was in sight just a couple blocks away. It would take forever to get there. He was looking inside the window of a bank thinking he could rob it. There was a pawn store too, but no guns and no ammo. He moved on. *Why am I doing this?* He tried to think of things he didn't like about Jeanine. Being a zombie was the main thing, that and beating him at foosball. Her snorting laugh was annoying, but her giggles were cute.

"This time I'm gonna do it. I can do it. I can kill her. I'll — kill — it!"

He tried to think of the last thing he killed. His face was a knot of concentration. *I killed a squirrel with a pellet gun once. Oh...*

"Yeah, I killed zombies." Those zombies had been friends and family. He could see their ghoulish faces coming after him. He killed them...so why couldn't he kill Jeanine? Maybe it was because the bat seemed like such an inhumane device. It was also a symbol of the best times they had together on the softball field. He kept moving and began to sob. For all he knew, the last one he would ever love was inside the building. He sighed just before he walked inside.

He entered the front door, stepping over the broken glass. The crackling underfoot stirred the hairs on his back. He didn't hear anything as he closed his eyes. He pictured Jeanine inside the cell as she had always been. He saw her standing there, a smiling tomboy with freckles and a nice body for a tall girl. If God had a woman in mind for him, it was Jeanine.

He exhaled and stepped inside the dim corridor. He made his way down the hall, breathing heavily. He wiped the sweat from his face with his shirt. There she stood, in the middle of the cell, facing the sunlit window in the back. Her dark hair flowed down over her neck. Her jean shorts were riding up inside her full rear. *Is that cellulite?* He shook his head. Her shadowed figure seemed perfect. His heart pounded. *Can it be?*

"Jeanine," he whispered.

The figure turned in slow motion. Her gored shoulder and dangling arm stopped his heart. The sunken black eyes were like deep wells, and the drooping jaw seemed to hang near the floor. *No–No–No!* It was all the same, only the day had changed. He looked down at the floor and all he could hear was a raspy breathing sound. A half-filled bowl of green soda lay on the floor. *That's interesting.*

The bowl was filled when he left yesterday. Another full bottle sat on the cot. *She didn't drink much.* Lost in thought he didn't notice she crept up to the bars.

"Num-Num."

He leaped back, almost falling to the floor. A fresh burst of pain lanced through his foot and leg. It was killing him.

"Geez Jeanine, you scared the shit out of

me!" he yelled back, swinging the bat into the bars.

"Num-Num."

"Go get your num-num! Dumb! Dumb!" *Oh, that's funny. Idiot!*

Her face was lost like an abandoned child's. The glassy black eyes were widened, without understanding. She backed away from the bars and began to kneel at the bowl. As Nate watched in disgust, something pricked at his ears. He moved back down the hall.

There was a different sound in the distance. He heard dogs barking from somewhere as he tilted his neck and shut his eyes. He looked back at his girlfriend, who was making loud lapping and slurping sounds. He headed toward the front door and stopped again. The sound grew louder and more distinct in his ears. Whatever it was, it was coming his way. A burst of energy empowered him.

He made his way into the bright sun and looked above. The noise seemed to be coming from the sun itself. He shaded his eyes with his hand and looked around. Louder and louder, the sound came. He saw a black speck appear in the sky. It got bigger with each passing second. He loved Vietnam movies and he knew that sound. *Is that a helicopter?*

"I can't believe it's a freaking helicopter!" he yelled as he hopped up and down, crossing his arms and bat high in the air. He was frantic with joy. It soared over his head bringing a whoosh of air, almost knocking him to the ground. He could see heads peering down at him from two hundred feet above.

"Come down! Come down!" he shouted.

The helicopter looked like an enormous bird of prey. It rounded over the town a couple more times and lowered itself to the street.

...THUWMP! THUWMP! THUWMP! THUWMP! THUWMP! THUWMP! THUWMP! THUWMP! THUWMP! THUWMP! THUWMP! THUWMP!...

The noise was music to his ears. It might as well have been angels who came out of it, once it landed. It was people, people in uniform, and Nate couldn't believe his eyes. An impeccable man in a blue Air Force uniform with silver stars on his shoulder shouted over the roaring helicopter.

"Are you Nate McDaniel?"

"Yes!" he screamed.

"Are you sure?" the man said, his hand on Nate's shoulder yelling in his ear.

Nate fumbled for his wallet in his back pocket and pulled it out to show the man. The officer tipped up his sunglasses and gave it a good look. The man slapped him on the shoulder; a broad smile was on his face as he gave a thumbs up to the men behind him. The soldiers in camouflage returned the signal.

The man yelled back in his ear saying, "Guess what Nate?"

"What!"

"You're a hero!"

"I am?" he yelled, feeling confused. "Why?" He read the man's name tag. *Dotson.*

"Son," the officer grasped his shoulders tight, "you sent the tweet that saved the world!"

"I did?"

The officer nodded and began looking around. "Say, where's that zombie?"

"What?"

"The zombie!"

"Inside there," he pointed back towards the sheriff's office. General Dotson pointed to his men. Two soldiers with M-16's headed inside, followed by a smaller man in black with a moustache, dark glasses and a shotgun. Nate shook his head. Something was going on.

"Hey — what are they doing?'

The general pulled at his arm, ordering him, "Stay here son!"

Nate jerked his arm away and ran back toward the building. *Jeanine!* Every step felt like a nail was being driven in his leg as he ran inside. He rounded into the hallway and faced a rifle barrel lowered into his chest. He kept going. Jeanine's face was pressed to the bars. The wiry man in black had the shotgun pointed in her face.

"NOOOO!" Nate screamed.

KA-BOOM!

He watched as her body fell lifeless onto the cell floor. He sunk to his knees gawping. Two hard-faced soldiers grabbed him under his arms and dragged him back outside. He couldn't feel a thing. The wiry man with the shotgun lit up a cigarette as he walked by.

Nate said, "Th-that was my girlfriend." He could see his reflection in the man's dark glasses. He could make out two beady eyes as well.

The man leered at him, and with a deep southern accent said, "*Was,* is the key word son."

CHAPTER 7

Guthrie, West Virginia

THE ROAD WINDED UPWARD, ACROSS a picturesque landscape of turning leaves and tall pines. The morning dew and lifting fog coated the grassy grounds along the way. The minivan with balding tires accelerated, screeching up the hill. The radio commercials droned on between breaks of blathering talk radio hosts. It was another big day, the annual celebration of the day Nate McDaniel saved the world.

The van screeched as a small buck came into view, leaping away from the honk.

"Stupid deer," the driver muttered as he stepped down on the gas. He hated this road. It was a long unkempt disaster filled with pot holes and mud. He could never keep the van clean, even during the dry summers. Why should he care? It was a company car. He had brought his cherry red muscle machine up once, his first day, and busted a rim. He hated the dreadful hill ever since.

Mile after mile, he suffered the gushing praise about Nate McDaniel, the man who saved the world. *With Mountain Dew or whatever.* He had roomed with Nate in college, the two of them had even pledged in the same fraternity. They had good times and a few bad. He squeezed the wheel. His roommate never cracked a book or went to class. Nate was bright, lucky and lazy. He always hated that about Nate, the ne'er-do-well. There was something else he didn't like either. Nate was a notorious liar who led a charmed life.

Here it comes, here it comes! A smooth spot of black top flattened up ahead, with several bumps rising in the road. He jammed on the gas.

"Yah-hooooo!" he cheered as the muffler dragged sparks over the exhilarating bumps and clanked the cargo in the back. It gave him a rush. He braked hard, entering a hairpin turn, and shot back up the hill, straddling a snapping turtle in the road. *The next one won't be so lucky.* Something on the radio caught his ear.

"Up next hour, Nate McDaniel will be joining us, celebrating the 6th year anniversary of when he saved the world," the speakers blared.

He switched it off, shaking his head. *That son-of-a-bitch couldn't save a cat from a tree with a ladder and a fireman.* Of course, having Nate as a friend had its benefits. It had been this same old roommate, the aspiring biologist and doctor of bullshit, turned savior of the world, that called and offered him his current assignment...and the pay was great. He allowed himself a smile as he thought about his 401k.

He hadn't seen his old roommate since college. It seemed like a lifetime ago. The private college hosted lots of academic challenges and a few interesting women. Nate somehow landed the goddess of the geeks in Jeanine. He never understood that relationship – or what happened to her six years ago, for that matter. *Charmed life.*

He approached a weathered structure that was fenced in. Fallen leaves covered the ground and rooftops of the old government building. Green moss and ivy decorated the walls and gutters. It was early in the morning on the hilltop, but it might as well have been night. He passed a blue sign on the road that read in gold letters: GUTHRIE FACILITY/ WEST VIRGINIA. It wasn't his favorite place in the world. As he looked ahead, he saw the high trees that choked out most of the sunlight like jagged curtains.

The brakes squeaked to a halt as he pulled alongside a weathered guard shack. An older man in mirrored sunglasses stepped out alongside his car. The guard wore a starched green uniform and a shotgun was slung over his shoulder. He rolled down his window.

"Evening John," he said, sticking his head out the window with a faint smile.

The man strolled around the car with agonizing slowness, checking his decals and looking in the windows. Another guard half the man's size appeared, shirt half-tucked over a pot belly. The smaller guard began running a long bomb-detecting device under the van's frame. *Every single time.*

John the guard stepped alongside his window and stooped down. The man's weathered face had a whimsical look and his big calloused hands clutched the driver's window edge. His big head, full of thick white and gray hair, peered in the back of the van and withdrew. A tooth pick jutted under John's moustache and a frown crossed his face.

"State yer business civilian," John said, in a voice as country as a coal burning stove.

He cleared his throat.

"I've come to kidnap the princess."

The man's eyes widened as he a gasped and said, "You best get a nicer chariot Sir Lancer Lots. Ain't no princess going nowhere with you in this thing."

John kicked the door.

"Maybe you should settle for Fergie over here."

John jutted his thumb toward the dumpy little guard.

He looked over and saw it was John's grandson, in a uniform sewn by his wife. The boy was about ten, heavy, with his chubby face scrunched up in a sneer. *It looks like the boy still has some pit-bull in him.* He knew that little Ferguson wasn't fond of working with his grandpa. It was that time of the year when mommy and daddy unloaded the boy while they committed consensual adultery.

"Hi Ferguson," he said, with a wave that drew the boy's tongue. *You have no resemblance to your father.*

John the guard asked in his usual cheerful voice, "So what's new Henry. Did you enjoy your time off?"

"Sure John, the cruise was wonderful, even with all the work, rain and lack of sunshine," Henry replied.

"That's too bad. Did you get me any taffy? I don't see any," John said, wringing his hands, licking his moustache.

"I didn't think you could have taffy. Remember what it did to your dentures the last time."

John's smile was bright white, "My teeths are just fine. Now, give me some taffy, or you ain't going in."

Henry opened the center console and pulled out the splashy box and handed it over. The boy bounced on his toes by the van's side. John inspected the box as a look of satisfaction crossed his face.

"You're alright Henry. I'll let you in I guess."

"Gee thanks, I can't wait. Anyone in there I should know about," he said, bringing the van in gear.

John rubbed the side of his face.

"Nah...it's just the usual suspects. I keep thinking there is something I need to tell you. You'd think if something new happened, I'd remember. It's just the same faces every day. Well, if I remember I'll give you a ring," John said, giving him a salute as he stepped inside the guard shack.

Henry watched the man press something that made a loud buzz and the gate slid open, shaking and rattling over the ground. He waved back as he pulled through. He heard John holler from behind as the gate began to close.

"It's your brother! Your brother's in there!"

A chill went down his spine. *What!?*

CHAPTER 8

THE FLUORESCENT LIGHTING HUMMED ABOVE as determined footsteps echoed down the corridor. The old facility was built like a block limestone prison and smelled like bleach. The shining elevator door waited ahead, a red light shining like a beacon above it.

Holding a box in his hands, Henry rose up on his toes and brushed the scanner with his back pocket. Nothing happened. He set down the box and pulled out his wallet from the back of his pants, and slapped it to the scanner. Nothing happened. Shaking his head, he pulled out the magnetic security card and tried again. The red light switched to green as he snatched up the box and got inside.

Up he went, coming to a stop after only one floor. As the doors parted, he stepped out into a lobby. An abandoned receptionist desk greeted him. The surrounding offices and cubicles were without life or light. *Good.* He hated the small talk, especially with the handful of people he worked with in the dreary place. A scent of coffee hung in the air. *I hope it's fresh. I wonder who is here?*

He headed toward the back, stepped inside his office and set the box on his desk next to a picture of him, his brother, dad and mom. Looking around, he noticed things were out of place and his fridge was cracked open. He looked inside.

"Jimmy!"

His drinks were gone, every last one of them. He thought about his younger brother and the problems he caused. During college, when the zombies came, Jimmy had gone into mental decline. Jimmy was only a year younger, and seemed to take all of his frustrations out on him. Jimmy's issues were only a nuisance at first; however, the past couple of years the issues had become quite problematic. And now, Jimmy was back, causing Henry to simmer within. *Why can't we get rid of him?* Henry had no idea what he'd done to deserve a brother like his.

There was a rustle of clothes behind him and he twisted around. Nothing was there. He stepped into the hallway. Somewhere in the room fingernails were tapping on a desk or counter top. The office area wasn't big enough for twenty workers, but he still had trouble locating the sounds. He squinted, scanning the room. *Who in the world?*

He felt his chest pocket and remembered

his glasses were still in the mini-van. He had plenty of trouble seeing without them and it made him uneasy. An office chair groaned from inside one of the cubicles. Turning his head, he backed up on his tip-toes, looking over the partition walls. A ghost-like voice whispered from somewhere close inside the room.

"Oh Henry..."

Oh my!

"Oh Henry," someone said again, closer than before.

He headed toward the source, step by step. He jumped out in front of a secluded cubicle.

"Gotcha!"

A black flat-screen monitor greeted him.

"Huh?" he said, scratching his head.

He started to turn around as claws dug into his side, driving him into the ground. A woman whispered as she chewed on his earlobe.

"Oh Henry! Oh Henry!"

It began to tickle now, as he burst out in laughter. He couldn't catch his breath as he tried to fight the soft belligerent figure accosting him.

"Stop!" he cried. "Stop!" He saw a thick tussle of brown hair as he shoved her back into the desk.

"Ouch!" she cried, bumping her head.

He gasped. "I'm sorry!" he said, reaching over, but she bounded onto his chest, tickling him again.

"You're gonna pay now Henry! Henry!"

He strained, trying to defend himself. She was groping him all over now. The tickles began to subside and turn into something else. They both were out of breath when he got his first good look at her. Her pretty round face had an alluring grin. Underneath an open lab coat her buxom figure was enshrined in lacy maroon lingerie and high black heels. Her heavy breasts wanted to burst out of her bra.

"Miss me?" she said as she straddled him, pinning his arms back behind his head. Her perfume was vitalizing. He was conquered.

"Words could never describe my longing for you?"

She slammed his hands back again.

"Is that a *yes* or *no*?"

"Yes Tori! Yes! Now get off me before someone comes."

She wiggled her hips on his.

"I'm pretty sure you don't want that...Oh Henry." Her voice was like honey. She was right, but he was chicken.

She looked around.

"No one's coming. It's just me and you."

She winked at him.

He tried to squirm, but she squeezed his wrists and her voice was like poison.

"Did you cheat on me?"

Oh no! Not this again. "No never!" He hadn't, either. "Of course I want you, but my creepy brother is here," he whined, "and—"

She sealed his mouth shut with a powerful kiss and began sucking on his tongue. She nibbled and licked his ear. "They're in the basement, so just relax and let me take care of you," she whispered. He did. Tossing off her lab coat she unbuckled his belt along with his pants. As she jerked his pants down below his knees the elevator chimed.

"Crap!" he said, wiggling away.

"What are you doing?"

He tried to whisper as he said, "Didn't you hear that — it's the elevator!"

"You're being paranoid."

She leaned onto his shoulders, her fragrant hair covering his face. Grabbing her shoulders, he pushed her off and fixed his clothes. Tori sat back, biting her lip and blowing the hair from her face. More lights came on above them and her face lit up. They looked at each other and scrambled.

He stood up, peeking over the low wall of the cubicle as she looked for her lab coat. They heard someone very close by, sucking the bottom fluid from a cup with a straw. He couldn't see anyone though. He needed his glasses. Several silent seconds passed as he motioned for her to stay put as he headed into the office, looking around. *Who in the—*

Tori shrieked as he jerked around just in time to see her crouched behind a chair. Goose bumps were all over her half-naked figure. A lanky man with a crooked ball cap and watery eyes hung over the partition wall. The man was laughing, shrill and creepy.

"Nice outfit Tori. How'd you know that's what I like," Jimmy said in a disturbing voice, while dangling her lab coat.

Tori darted behind Henry, clutching his waist.

"Go away you pervert!" she yelled.

Tori hated Jimmy. He hated Jimmy. Everyone hated Jimmy.

His brother climbed over the wall and sauntered over, pulling up his baggy pants and straightening his grungy lab coat.

"So, my prodigal brother returns."

"That would be you Jimmy," Henry said, snatching Tori's lab coat.

Jimmy was a twenty-something two-time college dropout who had failed to socially connect beyond middle school. He was smart, cunning and weasel-eyed. Henry couldn't stand the sight of him. *Why are you here?*

"What are you doing here Jimmy? I thought you were gone for good."

Tori began moving away toward the elevator, heels clopping on the floor.

"Bye Tori," Jimmy said, chuckling as she flipped him the finger. Jimmy wiped his nose on his sleeve.

"Pops said he needed some help, so here I am. I've taken over since you were gone."

CHAPTER 9

A LARGE GOLD AND BLUE CERAMIC coffee mug sat steaming on the break table. A black LCD TV hung from the wall, showing an aerial view of zombies being herded into a road sized tunnel. The view panned backward, exposing hundreds, growing to thousands, of morbid men and women inside miles of chain link fence. Security officers guarded the perimeter and forced the hapless people inside the tunnel.

Another video clip cut in, showing a billow of black smoke from a burning dump truck that had crashed along a highway. The gray and white ash remains of the zombies were spilled onto the blacktop. More security forces cleared the area, but they weren't quick enough to get all of the renegade footage. It was a scene from what happened in the years after Nate McDaniel saved the world.

Someone was tapping a spoon on their coffee mug in the room.

Tink. Tink. Tink.Tink.

Henry blocked it out, focusing on the scene above. Nate McDaniel's charming face appeared on the screen, again. Nate was busy recalling the events of his heroic situation to the television hosts that treated him like the President.

"Bugs ya, don't it," said a voice that crawled under his skin.

"You know me don't you," he said.

Jimmy took a sip from his mug and jerked back. "Ow! Damn coffee's hot!"

Really, idiot! "Why do you even bother? You never drink it." Henry was shaking his head as he pointed the remote, turning up the television.

His brother made another annoying sniff from his nose. It must have been the hundredth time in ten minutes. His mere presence made the walls close in, and the sound of his condescending voice made it worse. "Just trying to be like my big bro."

"Great. You are doing such a fine job, too." Sitting back on the break table, he studied the picture on the screen.

Jimmy started again, "Well—"

"Sssh!" He pointed his finger at the television.

Nate McDaniel was on the screen, tall and stylish, between two leggy reporters. *Nice Nate.* Nate looked as sharp as he'd ever been.

A gold cross was displayed around his neck. *He's got make up on.* Henry listened to the conversation on the television ...

"*So Mr. McDaniel, or should I say 'the man who saved the world', how does that scene make you feel.*" *The short-haired blonde reporter asked.*

"*Please, call me Nate.*"

"*Okay Nate. Take us back. Six years ago you sent a message that saved the world. Three years ago you began another quest — saving zombies. Tell us about that.*"

"*Well Julie, it's like this. What I discovered wasn't a cure, as people say. Rather, the caffeine and sugar combinations only suppressed zombie people's appetites for flesh and brains*".

The hungry-eyed woman hung on his every word.

"*We still need to find a cure so that the zombie people can live normal lives in the world, just like the rest of us. That is why I helped found the World Humanitarian Society.*"

A tan, long-haired brunette asked the next question, "*First Nate, I want to thank you. You saved millions, possibly billions of lives, and you seem to be on a noble quest to save even more.*" *She was shaking her head.* "*You are amazing.*"

He was grinning.

"Thanks Christy. But I don't deserve all the credit."

"Sure you don't," she added, squeezing his knee, drawing a look of disdain from her co-reporter.

"Tell us about the World Humanitarian Society, Nate," the blonde interjected, casting a quick glare at her counterpart.

"Oh, sure."

He began rubbing his hands on his thighs when the camera zoomed in for a close up.

"Well, like many of you, I also lost a lot of people I loved to zombieism. When I, I mean we, discovered a way to subdue their aggressiveness, we also learned there were other issues we needed to deal with as well."

The reporters sat engrossed at his side.

Fiddling with his cross, he continued, "Because the zombie people were so despised, we quickly began their incineration. And that clip" he motioned in the air," was one of our methods of paying them back for what they did to us. But after time, when the threat subsided, people like you and me started to wonder if our families were truly lost. People began trying to find their loved ones, wanting to bring them home, find a cure, and have resolution...even reconciliation."

"It certainly was an unforeseen blessing don't you think?" Julie the blonde asked.

Nate shifted in his seat as he replied,

"Absolutely. So many questions worldwide arose. Taxes, assets, debt, family, custody? Who was in charge of all of these decisions? Families? Governments? The zombies...er... zombie people?"

Christy the brunette added, "I remember going through all of this. It was horrifying. We had no idea where my brother and his wife were, and we got stuck with their children. I didn't know anything about parenting," she said with a shrug. There was a pause before Nate continued.

"So...the World Humanitarian Society stepped up, and with the blessing of the United States and the United Nations, they were able to facilitate the process of bringing order to the lives of the families and the zombie people. But—their main mission is to find a cure."

Julie reached over, patting his knee.

"And we know you'll find one, Nate."

"Nate, do you think the remaining z-people will get to vote?" Christy asked.

"Only if they're Democrats," he said with a subtle smile, causing a burst of unnatural laughter from both women.

"Tell us about your fiancé'" the brunette asked. Nate kissed his cross....

Henry shut the television off, tossing the remote on the table. *Ludicrous!* All the signs were there that Nate was lying: the sweaty palms and flickering eyes. He knew the story coming next. How he tried to save Jeanine from the zombies, and how they were trying to find a cure for her...somewhere.

"What do you think about all of that, Jimmy?"

His brother was stooped over, head inside the fridge saying, "I love Nate, man. He saved the world. Woo Hoo!" Jimmy added, arms raised high in the air. "I wish I was him. I'd be banging those two reporters right now."

Jimmy began humping the table, spilling Henry's coffee as he did so.

"Imbecile!" Henry snatched his cup from the table as the hot liquid stung his hand and almost spilled on the floor.

Jimmy stopped in motion, eyes frozen, then shouted, "I'm Nate McDaniel baby, I saved the world!" His brother started banging the table, using his fists like tom-tom mallets.

"What is wrong with you? Every day you have to jerk off! You create havoc! You leave a mess! You leave—you come back. Over and over again, like a rabid flea."

Henry set his coffee down and rolled his sleeves up as he rounded the table.

Jimmy hoisted his fists up. "Let's go bro!"

Henry caught his brother by the wrist and bent it downward, forcing Jimmy to his knees.

"Ow! That's cheatin'! Let go!" Jimmy cried.

He wouldn't. He wanted to break it. The look in Jimmy's distraught face gave Henry satisfaction. He fought the urge to kick in his ribs.

"You stay away from me and everyone—especially Tori! If I catch you leering at her again, I'll break your hands—got it!" He cranked the pressure up one more time.

"Yes," his brother said, writhing to the floor.

He let him go. How many times had they fought like this? He bailed his brother out time after time. Everyone did. That was part of the problem. Violence wasn't his style, but he was more than just a run of the mill scientist. He'd been a formidable ball player and runner in his day, too. Jimmy was nothing of the sort, just a pathetic life on legs.

Henry headed down the hall and scanned the elevator pad with his card. His stepped inside, and he could hear his brother laughing and sniffing. His brother was a risk, a dangerous one and he was back. There was only one way his brother could have got back in. It was time to check in with his dad. *Don't forget your glasses.*

CHAPTER 10

THE ELEVATOR CHIMED AS THE third floor button lit up and the steel doors slid open. Thirty feet down a hospital white corridor was another open room and entryway. The elevator doors began to close behind him as he started ahead. He noticed he was shaking as he stopped inside the entryway.

He stood inside the small square room and rubbed his shoulders. The facility was always cold. A set of lab coats lay on a shelf along the wall, and he slipped one on over his navy oxford shirt and beige dress pants. Another set of stainless steel doors awaited him. Above the door a red beacon loomed. He always wondered if, more than just a color, it was a warning.

On the white wall beside him he saw a plaque that read: **W.H.S., Guthrie WV Unit, Certification 111**. He pushed his glasses up the bridge of his nose and wondered if there was anything else he should have grabbed from the van. Beside the plaque was another rack filled with shotguns with synthetic black stocks. The sight of them gave him little reassurance compared to the days they kept armed guards at every door. Now there was less than a skeleton crew, one inside and John on the outside. *I wish they would finish that other elevator. Here we go.*

When he swiped his magnetic card, the green light flared and he watched the silver doors yawn open. He walked out into a vibrant room that only the most creative minds could have imagined. The sight was always unsettling, unnatural and impossible. The kaleidoscopic colors were intense and overwhelming. His chest tightened, and a cold sweat overcame him as he balled up his fists.

Inhale your sanity. Exhale the madness. Welcome back to the Zombie Day Care.

Small children's bodies were in slow motion, sputtering inside a rainbow room full of giant stuffed toys and radiant bean bag chairs. The bright clothes the children wore were in stark contrast to their olive gray skin and thinning hair. Near the middle of the room, a boy, about five years old, fell down a slide. A slack-jawed girl, maybe seven, stood in front of a large LCD screen, staring at an episode of Mister Giggle Pants. Another little boy wearing a red and white striped shirt was chewing the popcorn from the inside of a bean bag chair.

The words, "num-num," slowly escaped their gothic little lips, like a heartbeat. . The sound of soothing classical music did little to block out the eye-jolting assault on Henry's senses. Henry watched a little girl in a pink dress, still with much of her blonde hair, walking on a treadmill at an agonizing pace. He looked at the machine's timer: sixteen hours thirty-five minutes. *She must have just started.*

He looked up, searching for people in lab coats, working along the platforms and catwalks surrounding the room from above. No one was there. He walked deeper into the playroom, careful to avoid the children. He watched one child in a bright yellow Juicy Fruit shirt make a wide yawn. He steered clear of that one, as the sight of its gray teeth tingled his fingertips. *They're still dangerous.* But many of the others in the lab didn't share Henry's sentiments.

A voice shouted from above, "Hey, Sam Becket's back! Welcome back Dr. Becket!"

There was a small applause coming from somewhere on the catwalk above.

Shielding his eyes from the bright lights overhead he yelled back, "I'm not Dr. Becket... quit saying that."

"You look like him though," the same voice said.

"No, I don't. I have black hair and glasses." Henry pointed to his rectangular spectacles.

He watched a heavyset man traverse over the catwalks with loud footsteps to stand over him.

"You sound like him."

Shaking his head he pleaded, "I don't *sound* like him either. Can we please stop doing this?"

The man above was a few years older than him, with thick black hair, an unkempt beard, and meaty arms like sailor.

"Not until you say it," the man said in a determined voice.

"Say what?" He knew what.

The man was nodding his head, hairy arms folded over his belly saying, "You know what."

It seemed like every eye was on him now, but he couldn't tell from the lights. A little zombie child approached, causing him to step further away.

"We're waiting," the man said with his arms outstretched.

He held his finger up and the man above pressed his arms out while leaning forward on the rail saying, "Make sure we all can hear it."

He put his hands on his hips and said, "Oh crap!"

"Yes!" Rudy shouted. "Yes—you nailed it!"

A polite applause from another pair of unseen hands erupted inside the room. The man above him began climbing down a tunnel ladder that was similar to a building fire escape. The husky man dropped to the ground, stumbled, and fell face first into a bright green bean bag. Jumping up, the man jogged over and gave him a hug.

"I'm glad you're back Sam...I mean Henry!"

"Okay, okay Rudy, enough."

He squirmed away, looking around as another zombie boy was walking away.

"You act like I've been gone all year."

As Rudy stepped back, Henry could see the weathered Quantum Leap T-Shirt inside his lab coat. His friend must have everything the show ever made. Henry had even bought him one of those shirts for Christmas.

A thrill was in Rudy's voice as he talked, "Man! I–am–glad–you–are–back! It's never the same around here when you're gone. It's like a morgue."

"It is a morgue."

"Good one Bawk. Anyway, when your brother showed up right after you left—"

"Wait a minute," he grabbed Rudy by the shoulder, "When? *Right* after I left?"

Rudy turned a little pale, averted his stare and said, "The next day."

He's been here two weeks. How? Why didn't anyone say something? Tori? Rudy?

"Why didn't anyone tell me?" He was angry.

"Man, you sound just like him."

"Who? Jimmy?"

"No dude, Scott Bakula."

He rolled his eyes and grabbed his dumpy friend again. "Why didn't you guys tell me?"

The blustering man's eyes widened when he brushed his hands away and said, "Because we knew it would upset you, and we didn't want to ruin your vacation."

"Rudy," his voice was rising, "there are things more important than my vacation and that would be the safety of all these people." Rudy's head was down. Henry felt something brush along his side causing him to half-jump away. He exhaled, it was Tori.

"You mad at me too, Lover?" Her voice was sweet as honey.

"Yes!" he said as he straightened his glasses, climbed inside the steel ladder tube and huffed up the rungs.

Rudy was pointing at Tori as he mouthed the words; *I told you he'd be mad.* The two followed him up as Rudy tried to prompt Tori to go first, but she pushed him along ahead of her.

"Almost," he said, snapping his fingers.

The catwalks crossed over a platform that encompassed the outer rim of the day care.

The entire layout made him feel like he was on the set of an eighties spy movie. Computers and monitors were displayed along the walls and behind partitions. Some other familiar heads popped up and sunk back down behind their stations. It was the usual lukewarm reception at best. Watching zombies all day for a living did little for social development. *Where's Dad?*

Spying another set of doors along the wall, he headed for it with determination. *I bet he's in there.* More footsteps came from behind him, clamoring over the metal walkway. A warm delicate hand caught up with his, slowing him down.

He pulled away, but it held him tight.

"Let go Tori. I've got to see him."

She barred his way with her body, chest out, hands on hips.

"Don't be mad. Settle down, we've got something to show you." She pressed closer. "Just give us a minute."

Two heads of black hair were peeping over their monitors, with grins resting below.

Rudy's heavy hand slapped his butt saying, "Come on Bawk, you gotta see this!"

He couldn't imagine it was anything good, but their voices were filled with excitement. Tori's suggestive smile subdued his sense of dread, and Rudy's wild expression raised his brows.

"Okay, but can we drop the Quantum Leap bit. I don't look like him."

She grabbed his chin, "But you do sound like him...it's very sexy."

"Man, if you looked like him, you'd have it all," his friend was saying, pulling at the picture on his shirt.

"I'm better looking than that guy."

Tori was fingering a lock of his hair when she said, "It's okay Lover, nobody looks better than a movie star."

He slumped a bit as she pulled him down the platform. A small overlook stepped out and above a smaller multi-colored room below. A thickset boy, almost five feet tall, walked around the room at alarming speed for a zombie. A crop of medium brown hair hung down over its sunken eyes. The boy rushed around on brick heavy feet, elbows and knees stiff as boards as it rammed into a padded wall. The big boy fell onto the floor, only to pick itself up and rush again.

"What the hell!" Henry said, pulling his glasses up and glaring at Tori, then Rudy. "How did this happen, Rudy?"

"I don't know, I'm not a biologist, I'm just a watcher and recorder. GS-16, Dude." Rudy waived his ID that was pinned to his white coat in Henry's face. "Now check this out."

Henry knew full well that Rudy did know, he just didn't want the credit for it.

Rudy pulled a red rubber ball from a black canister and hurled it upside the zombie child's head, bringing forth a grunt. It turned and chased after the ball. Henry's breath stopped as it picked the ball up. *This can't be.* An uncomfortable thrill raised all his hairs from head to toe. The slack-jawed face below showed mild curiosity before its face contorted. The ball began to bulge while the child squeezed it like a bear would. It was grunting, trying to dig its clipped nails deep into the rubber. Neither the ball nor the zombie yielded.

"He'll play with that ball for hours, unless he bites it." Rudy was enamored by the scene, while Henry went over and grabbed Tori by her wrists.

"How long?" he said with disbelief.

"About a week," she said in a nervous voice. "Your dad told us to just observe. That's all we've done. It'll be alright Henry, relax. We're getting closer to a cure."

There is no cure. There is no good in this. Why! Why! Why!

He could never understand how after just a few years people seemed to forget that the zombies were within days, maybe hours, of wiping out the human race. Instead of destroying the menace, they wanted to cure it. It was insanity. There was no good to be had in zombies, no matter who they used to be. No one listened to him these days. At least no one important did, anyway.

"Watch this! Watch this!" Rudy yelled, almost falling over the railing.

The grayish child bit into the rubber, teeth tearing it like a piece of chicken. The ball deflated along with Henry's excitement. Another chill went down his spine as long dead images arose in his head.

"Are there any others?"

"No," Tori and Rudy both replied.

"Good. Where is my dad?" he demanded, looking at the doors to the micro-lab. Instead, they pointed below, meaning the basement. Henry knew he had to put a stop to this. Before it was too late.

CHAPTER 11

A WALL OF MONITORS DISPLAYED THE interior activity of the facility, inside and out. Many of them were without a picture, showing only a black screen or a green error message. Fingers tapped into a keyboard as the remaining views above switched back and forth.

The rest of the room was dark, featuring a low electronic hum and empty office chairs. Three security stations were there, but only one was occupied. There was a set of lockers, a small table, some cobwebs and a refrigerator. Along the wall was a half-empty gun rack below a gray locker that read AMMO. The dust was more modern than the equipment, but it would do. This facility was only a satellite agency, one of many, diminishing in funds and employees.

Guthrie was an old government building that was easy to hide, located in a high place no one cared to remember. When the zombie infestation was curbed and the World Humanitarian Society was created, there was a dire need for zombie care. Guthrie was an abandoned West Virginia state facility that was easier to conceal than modify. It was one of the first of its kind. The politicians in Washington, D.C. who had zombie family members were the first to hide the ones they loved, rather than incinerate them. The children were considered the least dangerous among the afflicted, so they were taken in first.

The first couple of years, many of the powerful slipped unnoticed up the swerving hill to visit Guthrie. However, the change in the seasons brought changes in offices, and those visiting privileges were revoked. None of them seemed to care though; there was no fervor about it. The zombie children were none the wiser. If their families had stopped caring, it was never missed by their kids. The funding was. Guthrie was on its last legs, a metal tomb decaying in the hills, soon to be taken by the greenery and forgotten.

Candy wrappers and crushed beer cans lay scattered on a black desktop, along with a credit card. A jittery hand began dicing up lines of white powder. A crisp green bill was rolled up. One by one the lines disappeared from the desk into the green tube, in long heavy sniffs. *It's not crack, but I still like it.*

Jimmy sat back, wringing his nose as he opened up his eyes in observation. Things became perfect, crystal clear. He was ready for anything now, his brother be damned.

Jimmy had a mission, a secret one that no one but him knew about. They paid him, fed his need and promised there would be more. The government men were fools; he would have done it for free. The drugs were more than enough to see everyone suffer.

His shaking hands and dirty fingers became busy opening computer files and rebooting black screens. *This will be awesome!* Standing up, he powered up digital recorders beneath the monitors, bringing the sounds of more whirs and whines.

He spun around a few times, humming a demented tune. Jimmy flopped back down in his chair, his gaze transfixed on some figures on a particular screen. Jimmy observed Henry, Rudy and Tori standing in wonder at the sight of Louie in the kid cave. Anger rose inside him as he watched his brother's commanding presence control his stooges. His brother was a tall, lean figure with jet black hair and soft features. Henry's vivacious girlfriend seemed spellbound by his words.

Jimmy didn't know why he hated his brother, he just did. The pair used to be inseparable. In high school, Jimmy realized he wasn't what his brother was — refined, athletic, and sociable. People made Jimmy uncomfortable. People were cruel, and they didn't understand him. He tried to fit in, but he just didn't. They teased him. As smart as he was, no matter what he tried, he still lived in Henry's shadow.

Jealousy consumed him for years. The zombies came and his bad habits became worse. He never realized it was the drugs that rattled his mind and embellished his delusions. The little devils of his conscious always suggested Henry stood in his way to raging success. He no longer recollected that they had been best friends at one time. They used to hunt, fish and crack game codes days on end. Even after high school they were still at it. When the zombies came, their violent struggle for survival managed to put an end to all of that. Somehow it was all Henry's fault in his mind.

Henry. Henry. Henry. Sometimes he was torn by love and hate, but not for long. His plan should have taken place already, but it proved more difficult than he anticipated. He pounded his fist over and over again on the desk. Henry's look of concern troubled him. *He's always worried about something.* Henry never let him have the kind of fun he wanted. Henry never trusted him, and he would be hard pressed to succeed with the protector around. He almost had what he wanted now. *He can't stop me now. It will be too late.*

He didn't notice he was shaking and sweating as he watched his brother leave the screen. Tori and Henry were arguing back and forth when Tori stormed away. Jimmy began laughing under his breath, a wicked one, followed by another deep sniff. He wiped his sleeve along his nose thinking about what he had to do next.

Clicking his mouse, he opened folders, one by one, until he came to a folder reading TORIHOT. Inside it were several tori.wav files beckoning to be opened. Launching number 17 he became excited. There she was, splendid as a daisy working at her desk, breasts heaving inside her tight black dress. *You'll be mine soon, baby doll.* He leaned back as he unzipped his pants.

CHAPTER 12

Washington DC

NATE McDANIEL HAD TROUBLE SLEEPING. It was the time of year where the interviews and the past wore his mind down. Saving mankind had its benefits: fame, fortune and a never ending line of willing companionship, but none of that cleared his conscience. The truth was something that had little meaning to him back then, but now he became obsessed with it.

An eighty inch Plasma TV showed a variety of pictures as he lounged on his soft leather sectional. News, sports, Facebook, Twitter, and other sites were active, along with the voices from ESPN radio. A wireless keyboard sat in his robed lap, and a half empty glass of orange juice sweated on the lamp table at his side. A soft figure was huddled in the corner of the sectional, snoring softly. She was dark haired, and wearing lime-colored lingerie. He couldn't recall her name. *Julie? Christy?*

Danielle? She was a talk show anchor, one of the best. If the audience only knew what a freak she was.

He laid a cotton blanket over her. She rustled. *Oh no.* She lay back down, continuing her snores. *Good.* It was time to obsess on the truth again as he began to learn what guilt was. Jeanine entered his thoughts a lot this time of year. No therapy could remove the image of her hapless face being splattered across the tiny jail cell. The ringing blast of the shotgun woke him up in a cold sweat countless nights. *That little man in black.* He hated him.

The killer's uncompassionate viperous face haunted his thoughts. Fate entwined him with that man, who could be seen in the background of many interviews he caught on the web. He never got his name, but he was there, armored in dark glasses and a chiseled expression. He took a sip of juice as he reviewed the headlines on the plasma screen.

WHS CLOSE TO ZOMBIE PEOPLE CURE

ZOMBIE PEOPLE TAKE OVER VILLAGE IN SOUTH AFRICA

SOUTH BEACH WOMAN CLAIMS ZOMBIE PERSON INPREGNATED HER

GOVERNMENT OFFERS NO EXPLANATION TO ZOMBIE DISAPPEARANCE

MAN CHARGED WITH HATE CRIME FOR KILLING ZOMBIE WOMAN

ZOMBIE VACCINE TESTED IN AUSTRALIA

MYSTERIOUS ZOMBIE CARE DEATHS IN ATLANTA RAISE QUESTIONS

Every day he did more research, contacting a few sources under anonymous profiles. The list of conspiracy theories had grown for years, but now it had begun to dwindle. A few of them began to make sense. The biggest question that no one asked any more was: Where did the zombies come from? It bothered him day and night.

He was now the poster boy for the World Humanitarian Society, but that was all. He was given a script and told to stick to it. Jeanine, according to his handlers, was his inspiration for finding a cure. They had convinced him to go along with this by giving him the firm impression that he didn't have a choice. He played along just like he always did. He even lied to her family about how it all ended. He was a coward, but he was no longer used to it.

He got up, ignoring the biting pain in his stiff knee, and pulled some curtains back. The sunlight began to fill the room with a soft glare. It was Saturday, his date's day off. *Christy. That's it.* He cast another glance the woman's way, but she hadn't moved. He gave a sigh of relief, and limped from the living room in his Washington, D.C. condominium. A loud space tune jingled from the kitchen. Pain stabbed him below the knee as he bolted over and snatched at his smart phone. He missed, and it dropped with a loud thump into the metal sink, still ringing. He got a hold of it and answered in a soft voice, "Hello."

The voice was blaring on the other side.

"Good morning sir, how are you feeling?"

He held his hand over the phone, while looking over at Christy.

He tiptoed back to his bedroom.

"I'm fine. Why are you calling, Harry?"

"Just making sure you survived your big day. You and Christy made plenty of headlines last night."

He sat down on his bed, face drawn tight. "What? She was in a limo the whole time. She met me here. No one could have seen." He didn't see anything in the papers, but he hadn't been checking the tabloids either.

"Take it easy son, I'm just pulling your leg. Glad to hear you are alright. I'll let you get back to your day. Have a good one."

The line went dead. Nate's face was blank as he stared at the phone.

Every day, at any given hour, Harry or some other underling of the WHS would call. There was never a day without them. He hated it. They always seemed to know what he was doing. Rubbing his knee, he got up, checked his blinds, and scoured the ceilings and doorways with his eyes. He ran his soft hands along the mirrors and door frames. It was a habit. Despite all of his precautions, they still knew who he was with.

Inside the bathroom, he brushed his teeth, gargled and spit. He stared in the mirror, rubbed his grizzled face, and squeezed some blackheads on his nose. He combed his curly brown hair with his fingers and smiled at himself. *Not feeling it today.*

The day after his global celebration was usually filled with relief and relaxation. All of the planning and interviews from being '*The man who saved the world*' were done. He was still filled with anxiety, however. Someone sent him a link to one of his profile accounts. It led to another series of videos, articles and speculation...and they made sense.

He hung his white terry cloth robe behind the bathroom door, slipped out of his Darkslayer pajama pants and got in the shower. The hot water drilled deep into his hairy chest, steaming the bathroom glass.

"Ah," he said as he worked up a soapy lather.

He slipped at the sound of a rubbing squeak that came from the other side of the shower glass. He tried to rinse the soap from his eyes, only to open them to a burning sensation. *What in the....* A figure began to appear in the moisture of the glass. It started with an '*S*' and ended with an '*X*'. A perfect figure with a heart-shaped ass stepped inside.

"Good morning." Christy's voice was hotter than the water.

He watched the water soak her hair and cascade down her body.

"It certainly is," he said.

Christy erased all of his anxiety while another figure moved about the condominium with a gun. The cries and moans from inside the shower brought a smile to the man's crooked lips. The man made out the word on the shower door, nodded and walked away.

Minutes later, Nate stepped out of the shower and could have sworn someone had been there. On the floor, an imprint of a shoe appeared on the wet tile, but Christy stepped right through it. He looked at the carpet and noticed nothing strange.

"What's wrong," she said, staring up into his eyes and wrapping her hands around his neck.

He hoisted her up and tossed her onto his bed. "Nothing baby."

CHAPTER 13

Guthrie, WV

"**G**RANDPA," SAID LITTLE FERGUSON AS his pudgy thumbs worked his Gameboy, "...are you ever going to tell me what's inside there?"

John's grandson asked that question often over the years. The boy had been coming to work with him, once or twice a year, since he was six and now he was ten. John wasn't one to tell a lie, or make open assumptions. He just scratched the back of his neck, while gazing upward into the dim midday sky. What kind of story would he concoct this time around?

"Well Grandpa?"

A brisk wind was rustling the turning leaves, and the surrounding pines began to bend. He poured the last of his coffee from his battered metal thermos. He took a sip of the lukewarm substance, thinking about the daunting building inside the rattling fence.

The air felt cold in his lungs as he struggled to find the right words.

"Fergie, sometimes yer just better off not knowing. Besides, I can't really say for sure, and maybe that's the best for both of us."

He rubbed the boy's head with his rough hand.

"And I figure if the Lord wanted us to know, we'd know. I do know this, there are some good people in there, and I'd just assume that good things must be going on."

His grandson's head never came up, nose down in his video game. A few moments passed before John took another long swig of coffee.

Ferguson made a flat remark. "The kids at school say there are zombies in there."

He choked in mid-swallow and began to cough.

"You all right Grandpa?" He felt a small hand pounding on his back. He took another slug of coffee and began clearing his throat. He pulled his mirrored sunglasses from his weathered eyes.

"Who on earth told you that?"

"Teddy Knox...Jasmine Starks...Russell and his dad...lots of kids say it."

He honestly had no idea that zombies were in there, but he suspected it. The truth was, there had never been a zombie within a hundred miles of the place as far as he knew. But something about this facility never settled right with him. It wasn't long after they got the creatures under control that it was remodeled. He'd worked there when it was a state owned building, then the federal government took over, followed by the WHS. Sometimes people just knew things in small towns.

Everyone knew there were zombie cares all over, and where many of them were, but not all. For top secret reasons, certain situations were only "need to know," by those who knew. He'd waved many a dignitary through the gates from time to time, but still he did not know. He didn't want to, either.

John's voice was playful as he said, "Now, what makes you think they have any idea what is in here? They're just pulling your leg, trying to scare you."

His grandson growled as a deflating chime came from his game, and the boy snapped it shut.

"It says so on the Internet. They showed me a website."

"Did it scare you?"

Heck, the sound of thunder scared the boy, and he couldn't imagine him not being scared of zombies.

"Yeah...but I'm not scared anymore."

"Why not?" John was curious.

"I'm never scared when I'm with you, Grandpa."

John's mild eyes began to tear up as he gave his grandson a warm hug.

He studied the facility. Green beacons shown around the lower entrance and all along the fence. Well, they had. Now, many of the beacons were blacked out. *This place is going all to heck.* He could have sworn some of those lights flickered as the sun dipped below the tree tops, shadowing the outer gate in darkness. He couldn't shake the coldness. *This shift won't end soon enough.*

CHAPTER 14

RED. GREEN. RED. GREEN. THE basement was indistinct from the rest of the facility, cold and impersonal. More florescent lit corridors led from the elevator to a stairwell. As he made his way down the spiraling steps, an uneasy feeling set in again. Working upstairs was uncomfortable, but downstairs was downright claustrophobic. A red beacon awaited him at the bottom. It was time to get some answers. He sucked in his breath and scanned his card to open the metal doors.

A pale yellow light illuminated the room that had the makeup of a forensics lab. A pair of autopsy tables kept two small bodies at rest. Chlorine, vinegar, and other pungent smells filled his nose. A large black man was pulling green and white striped papers from a loud printer. The man quickly tore each sheet off and studied the results, pushing up his thick framed glasses.

Henry could hear, 'uh –huh', sounds

muttering under the man's breath. He watched as two big hands crumpled the large papers into a tight ball. The big man spun and shot the wad of paper over the autopsy tables. The ball of paper landed with a bang inside a metal trash bin in the corner.

"That's a three!" the man shouted in a deep voice, arms high, and fingers almost touching the high ceiling. Henry began a mild applause and the man lurched at the sound.

"Well, look who's back," the big man said, arms wide as he approached.

Oh no. He felt the man's arms wrap around him, pinning his arms as if he were a child. His feet left the ground for a long moment and his back cracked before he felt the hard floor again. Henry straightened his glasses.

"Do you always have to do that?"

"Of course...you're my boy," the man said, smiling. It was hard to resist Stanley's charm. The man was always positive, his face wizened and cheerful, with a soothing and powerful voice. Henry's anger had subsided, but not to the point he would not vent his concerns. As ingenious a scientist Stanley was, he still had his flaws.

"Dad, why on earth is Jimmy back here?" he said, raising his voice. "What are you giving to the zombies? Is what I saw with Louie the XT serum?"

Henry stepped towards the man and looked

up into his eyes, but Stanley turned away, shuffling papers on a desk.

"Don't worry about it, Son...you're always so serious. Come over here; we had a break through while you were gone."

Stanley draped his arm over Henry's shoulders and shoved him along between the autopsy tables. Two girls in pink and white striped sweat suits were strapped down. Their faces were ashen, eyes sunk, skin dry and grey. Black pupils rolled all over without a flicker of knowledge. Their hands and feet flinched from time to time. He expected some moans, but they were silent.

Careful to keep his distance from the edge, Henry stayed at the foot end of the tables.

"What is this? They aren't moving."

"They're dying," Stanley said in a sobering voice.

The words sent a jolt through his body.

"What happened? How do you know?" Henry said, studying the two girls.

His dad leaned against one of the tables, pulled out a cigarette and began to smoke.

"Well, one day they just stopped moving."

Stanley snapped his fingers.

"They stood for days before they fell down."

"Aren't Jill and Jean the oldest here?" he said, circling the metal tables and taking a closer look. He pulled an ophthalmoscope from his pocket and flashed a beam of light in Jean's eyes. The girl's pupils didn't shrink, which wasn't normal.

"Yep, but they were also afflicted earlier as well. These are the senator's grand girls. They've been in other facilities before."

Henry was still finishing college when all of this happened. The senator's family had made many visits, unlike the rest. Now that the senator was out of office, his contact with the girls had been lost. The family had signed off on the girls and ceremoniously buried their memory. Henry suspected the senator's influence had funded Guthrie, and now those funds were diminishing.

If other day cares had experienced zombies dying, he had not heard. If longevity was an issue, this might be the first case. It felt good knowing these creatures would eventually die. It gave him hope.

"How long have they been like this?"

"About a week," Stanley said, as he pointed the red dot of a thermal scanner at Jill. "Seventy-five degrees. It was eighty when I brought them down here. I am guessing when it hits room temperature they're done."

"Then what?" Henry felt a strange big of sympathy.

"Then, *the up and ups* said to cremate them."

The zombie girls were each hooked to a pulse and blood pressure monitor. The digital pulse figure was between 15 -20 beats per minute, compared to the usual 40 -50 bpm. The blood pressure readout was blank.

As his father blew smoke into the air, a hum and whir sounded and the wispy vapor was sucked into a vent above. The sound stopped. Stanley looked up, blew more smoke, and the sound returned, taking away the smoke, but the fans kept going.

"So, is the cremation chamber working?"

"Sure, that's where all the garbage goes."

It was a fitting end to the zombies. As far as he was concerned, they never should have stopped the genocidal disintegration. The zombies weren't people; they were flesh-eating life takers, the bottom of the food chain. He saw it first hand, and it still horrified him. If there was anything he could do to stop them he would, but the WHS wouldn't allow it. He kept those thoughts to himself.

He was deep in contemplation when he felt something brush against his lab coat. He let out a cry of alarm when he turned.

"Mom!"

She didn't reply. He backed up, facing her. Her curly red hair was in contrast to the metallic environment surrounding her. She was as tall as him, dressed in tight blue jeans and a brown wool turtle neck sweater. His nerves were on edge from the unexpected sight. It had been a long time since he had seen her. She opened her mouth to speak.

"Num-Num. Num-Num."

His heart collapsed in his chest. Her resemblance to the real thing had caught him off guard. She followed him around the table as he backed away, giving her a closer inspection. *She has a wig on!* Her clothes, painted nails and make-up increased the illusion of a real woman. Her cracked and sunken eyes, slack jaw and pasty hands reminded him she was still a zombie.

"What did you do?" he said, voice cracking. He was freaking out. She almost looked like someone he once loved. He fought an instinctive urge to hug her. "Why is she here running loose?"

"Henry...settle down," Stanley said in a reassuring voice. "She's as sweet as a kitty cat. Just look at her. She's still got that something, makes those jeans look just right...just like the first time I saw her."

He couldn't hide his bewildered look.

"That's sick Dad!"

"No son, that's love."

Stanley walked over and stroked her cheek.

"Num-Num."

It pained Henry's ears to hear his mother say that.

If he hadn't been certain before, he was now: Guthrie was his least favorite place in the world. His mother, Linda, wasn't home in West Virginia when the zombie outbreak came. She was at a teaching seminar in Houston, Texas. She had been one among tens of thousands of victims. It was a miracle when they found her days before her scheduled cremation. They had no idea where to look after months of searching. A news camera, of all the dumb luck, caught her face on the evening news at a controversial location in North Dakota. Stanley fought like a man possessed to get her back, but it was Henry who called in a favor, to Nate McDaniel.

Henry's irritation returned.

"Is that why Jimmy is back? If Mom dies, is he going to be a pall bearer?"

His palms and fingers fanned out, beckoning for an answer. His mom gave up on his brother long ago, but Stanley just never understood. Stanley gave Jimmy too many second chanccs.

Stanley shrugged and moved away from the argument, saying "He's family. He should have a chance to say good-bye. I never got that chance with my mom or dad. You don't understand. Just let it be; it will be over soon."

The sad look in Stanley's eyes told the rest. Henry watched Stanley give his mother a kiss on the cheek.

Stanley changed gears and said, "Are you

and Tori still getting on well? She's a fine looking lady. She reminds me of your mother."

Not this again. Please not this again. It was too late, as Stanley had begun the story of how he met his mother. Meanwhile, his mother walked away, bumping over and over again into a book case.

"I remember the first time I saw your mother. It was my first day as the assistant basketball coach at the middle school. Linda was coaching the cheerleaders. I never saw hair like that on a woman before ..."

"Hey Stan—" but Henry knew it was too late to stop him from talking.

"...I was down, and so was she. Your dad had just left her and you two boys. He went to Vegas to be a comedian, and lucky for me, he never made it back."

Henry buried his hands in his face. Telling the story kept Stanley from the reality he couldn't handle. Henry let his stepfather go on, knowing Stanley wouldn't stop now anyway. *Please don't talk about the honeymoon.*

"...Both my knees were shot from college ball, but Linda talked me into trying some classes. I told her if she went out with me, I would take classes. I loved playing ball, but if I'd never blown my legs out, I never would have realized what I could do."

Stanley tapped his head with his long finger.

"I ended up with a scholarship — in biology," Stanley said with a wry smile. "Man, a scholarship in basketball and biology. My mom would've died if she ever new. I'd almost forgotten how much I liked science when I was a boy. Mom bought me my first chemistry set."

Henry could recount the story word for word if he had to. Still he played along, mindful of his mother lumbering through the lab. It took about fifteen minutes of intermittent nods and *'uh-huh's'* before Stanley finished. The big man sat down at a metal desk chair and rubbed his knees as he watched his zombie wife. The exhausted expression on Stanley's round face stirred sympathy in Henry's chest.

Henry hated to say it, but he felt compelled.

"You can't bring back the dead, Dad."

Stanley's voice was solemn when he said, "Christ did."

"Yes, but he was God."

"The apostles did."

Stanley flicked a long ash on the floor.

"Dad," his voice was soft as he patted his stepfather's big shoulders, "you have to let this go. You look tired. How long has it been since you ate?"

"I'm okay. It's only been a few hours. Tori always brings me something down."

There was long moment of silence between

the two as the exhaust fans kicked off. Only the sound of Linda's shuffling feet remained.

"Okay. Let's go back to Jimmy and the XT Serum. Jimmy has to go—now! Remember the last time? Do you remember what my sick brother did to Jill and Jean?" he said, making a frantic motion towards the zombie twins strapped to the tables.

Jimmy did disturbing things to the girls, things Henry couldn't bring himself to speak of. Jimmy was a self-absorbed little minion who'd do anything for a laugh or a thrill. No one ever understood Jimmy's sick sense of humor.

His father was nodding; his face was in his hands saying, "I know, I know," Stanley whispered, "...I'll ask him to leave tomorrow."

"Try now! Or I'll do it."

"You can do it."

Some satisfaction filled him up. Getting rid of Jimmy would be the very next thing Henry would do.

"Now, what is going on with Louie upstairs? Is that the XT Serum?"

Stanley nodded, "I knew I should have waited."

Life started to fill Stanley's voice as he sat up.

"Take a look at this."

Stanley got up with a heavy groan and headed over to a computer screen.

Henry followed him and saw MRI head scans on the flat screens. One was cold: black, blue and gray. The other screen had flares of orange, green and red above the brain stem. He studied the data on the screen.

"This was three days ago?"

His stepfather was nodding.

"Who...Jill and Jean?"

Stanley pointed and said, "This one is Jean."

"But I thought they were dying."

"Well, as such, I thought they would be better subjects. I did both. Same results."

It was significant. Brain activity on a zombie was almost non-existent, but here there was something. As a scientist, Henry couldn't control his excitement. This was a big deal. All of these years in the facility had been spent dealing with children. Their brains were more apt to learn and absorb information. They relied more on instincts and had a stronger survival mode. Zombie children reacted to stimulus more often than adults. Their minds hadn't been polluted and their brain cells were still an incubator of growth. The zombie children shed the most light for hope of a cure.

"So how come they are still dying?" he asked with avid curiosity.

"There is only so much XT, and it was a

small dose at that. It lasted a day. The girls...
began walking again."

He pulled on his dad's shoulder and said,
"Does anyone else know?"

"Nah, I kept them down here." Stanley's
smile widened. "Think about it Son, with this
breakthrough we can get back our funding.
Maybe get a huge promotion."

"What about Louie? Is he on it?"

"One dose, every other day. Look at his
brain pattern."

Stanley toggled between the screens
and opened another file. One fourth of the
subject's brain above the lower stem was a
rainbow of color.

"Wow!"

They clasped each other's shoulders.
Things were getting better.

But someone else did know. The cameras
above had caught it all. He had been watching
all along. Jimmy knew everything and a gold
mine would soon be his.

CHAPTER 15

ER TUMMY GRUMBLED AS SHE entered the break room. All of the excitement from Henry's return flustered her. Bathed in the white refrigerator light, Tori rummaged through the shelves. Pulling out a box of pizza, she grabbed a roll of paper towels from the break room counter top. Opening the box she let out a disappointing moan. *Hawaiian? ...Oh, there's a piece of sausage.* She stuffed it in her mouth, chewing with a shrug. *What the heck.*

"Girl's got to eat," she muttered, placing three slices on a plate inside the microwave and hitting the PIZZA button. As happy as she was that Henry was back, she felt blue. So much had happened while he was gone, and she hadn't told him. Rudy and Stanley told her it would ruin his trip, but not telling him seemed to have ruined it all anyway. She wished she could have just gone with him on the cruise, something she had never taken before. Oh, what she would do for him on the open sea. His kind eyes and handsome face soothed her soul like no other man; even his serious demeanor didn't dissuade her efforts.

"Henry needs us girls," she said, hoisting her bra straps as she produced a jar of nail polish.

She checked her teeth on the rectangular mirror she had taped inside of a cabinet door and shot herself a wink. She pulled out a chair, took a seat and began re-painting her long black nails. She had just finished applying the last coat when the microwave chimed. She got up, took out the steaming pizza and tossed it onto the table. The strong smell of the pizza caused her stomach to groan again.

The room was quiet as she turned her back to the doorway and reached back inside the fridge. She felt eyes were burning on her lower back. Someone was there. She looked back over her shoulder hoping to see Henry, but only a black television monitor greeted her concerned glare. Back inside the fridge, two liters of leftover birthday soda were all she had to choose from. The one that read 'diet' got the honor. She froze before she pulled the bottle free. Her nerves were on edge, and all she could hear was the refrigerator's hum.

"Who's there!" she yelled, turning with the bottle held before her like a club.

The room was empty. Her made up eyes

darted back and forth. She stepped into the doorway and peeked outside into the main office. The cubicles and office were dark, where the overhead fluorescent lights were only on in part. She liked the dark, but not today. Along the outside of the break room, she began flipping on more switches, and the office became as bright as could be.

Sighing, she sat back down and said, "That's better."

Eating her pizza she checked out a copy of USA Magazine. Nate McDaniel was on the cover, and she wondered if she would get to meet him. Henry had told her a few interesting things about him. She found that man fascinating, but not as good looking as she hoped. Coughing on a big bite of pizza, she took several big drinks of the soda.

"Damn!" Still coughing as she went to the sink, she began drinking from the spigot. Something was stuck in her windpipe and she was hacking hard. It flustered her, but she got it washed down.

"Whew, that was scary."

She felt a pair of hands on her hips.

"Ah Henry, my hero, you came to save the day."

Turning to face him, she recoiled in horror, shoving Jimmy's leering face away.

"Son of a bitch!"

She rounded the other side of the table.

Men had pawed at her since she was thirteen, and she had learned to handle them, but this man gave her the willies.

"Ah come on Tori, it ain't like you don't want me," he said, followed by a heavy sniff. "Remember that time we went to the movies?"

The ball cap was twisted on his head, half covering his long grubby hair. She could see the dandruff flakes on the shoulders of his sports jersey. He looked her up and down, brown eyes wild with lust. The strong odor of alcohol mixed with sweat replaced her hunger with nausea. Jimmy's face had turned from good-looking, like his brother; to an unkempt miscreant no one wanted to know. Long ago, she had gone to the movies with him in school and she had been naughty. Now, she felt like all of those sins had caught up with her. Her knees were locked as he made his way between her and the door.

"Go away Jimmy," she managed to let it out. "That was a long time ago. I don't even remember it." She did remember it however, now it came back to haunt her.

"Well I sure do," he said on his approach.

He reached out and grabbed her cheeks in one big hand and squeezed them. She couldn't believe she wasn't moving. Some strange power kept her still. Something kept her near, something dangerous. His breath was on her neck and she felt him inhale her. He was like a snake when he whispered in her ear.

"Henry ain't got nothing on me girlie, and you know it."

Something inside her snapped. Her weakened will turned to iron as anger replaced her weakness. She launched her knee into his crotch. He groaned aloud as he sank to the floor, cursing.

"You bitch! You bitch! You bitch!"

She didn't hear a word as she ran away as fast as her legs would go. Tears were streaming down her cheeks as she entered the elevator. She felt exposed and worthless. She couldn't tell Henry; he wouldn't understand. She just had to keep it inside and pray Jimmy left soon. Or died.

She wanted out of this place, but didn't know where to go. The elevator opened into the parking garage and she ran for her car, shutting herself inside, hoping no one would miss her. It was a long time before she settled down. She was crying so loud that she almost didn't hear the elevator open. She crouched deeper into the backseat of her car and buried her head. She heard footsteps shuffling over the gravel close by, and she couldn't remember if she had locked the door.

CHAPTER 16

H E SAW COLORS AND HEARD sounds that were familiar. There were shapes and people, some moving and others not. Everything was new whenever he opened his eyes. A hunger and curiosity burned inside, but he didn't know what that was. Confusion and fear overwhelmed his senses, but it was all normal as far as he could comprehend.

A soft wall barricaded his path somewhere else. He moved along its side, tripping over plastic objects he didn't know were there. He fell, got up, and fell again. He didn't remember how many times he had done this. He didn't remember how many times he did anything. Things would go black and turn to color again. Every place he awoke was in different shades. Yellow, blue and gray surfaces coated his eyes.

Something sharp jabbed into him, but he felt no pain. More of those familiar looking things stared down on him. There were balls of many colors, filled with lines, triangles, circles and other shapes. Deep inside he felt he knew them, but most times they scared him.

Abandonment, loneliness and despair were emotions he did not remember. Flashes of other figures intermingled with his thoughts. He smelled things that made him hunger and his mouth watered. His bleak existence had no meaning, not to him. He traveled up something and slipped down it. A thrilling sensation overcame him. He wanted that again, but didn't know how. Something smacked him in the head. He saw it, round and red. He picked it up and said, "Numma-numma."

CHAPTER 17

SHE WAS STILL THERE, LYING like a baby sheep in a meadow. The plush mattress cushioned her curled up figure, snuggled in Nate McDaniel's silken sheets. No sound, no matter how abrupt he made it, stirred her excellent figure. She was exhausted, but not from him, as he would like to think, rather her demanding job with the media. He sat at her side admiring the woman he had just scored. Being the most famous man in the world had its advantages, all of which he knew he was not worthy of. Sighing, he covered up her naked figure, got up and walked stiff legged out of the bedroom.

Shaking his head he said, "I hate it when this happens."

She's still here. He couldn't stand that. She was one of *those* kinds that wanted to hang around, pick his brain or have a nice dinner in town. More press, more pictures, maybe a wedding...he understood the road she was on. He'd been trying to get off the celebrity highway for years, but it wasn't possible.

The seclusion of his high-rise condominium kept most wanton predators at bay. It was his three thousand square foot man cave. The starlets of his world came and went as he saw fit. This was his anti-matrimony lair. No girls allowed...for long.

He followed a short set of stairs into a den that overlooked the city of Washington, D.C.. Nate's study was plenty big, displaying custom mahogany cabinets, marble counter tops and an oversized mini bar. Closing the door behind him, he grabbed a Gobster energy drink from the fridge. Pulling back the tab, he glanced over the can. *Caffeine and sugar... the nectar of the zombies.* He let out a quick laugh; after all, it was his dumb luck that made the discovery. It seemed that two of his favorite ingredients were the zombies' as well. He felt an unsettling in his stomach and set the can down.

He watched the busy city streets below. The streams of people, as small as ants, seemed to be on the move as the rain began to splatter his window. He could never crush the thought that all of those people might have been zombies, should have been zombies, if not for him. Now, he wanted to be ready if it happened again.

The only good that came from the zombies

was the dismemberment of global terrorism. The Middle East was inflicted at the outset and their losses were reported heavier than most. Leaders of the tight knit networks all but disappeared, either from death or zombieism, as most speculated. Many differences were settled, as people all over the world seemed to understand that there were bigger problems that needed to be addressed...like extinction.

Sitting down in a comfortable leather desk chair, he checked some accounts, read messages and texted a few that had dangled in his thoughts for days. He felt like there were a thousand things he needed to do, but that wasn't the case. A thirty-six inch LCD was suspended before him. He spent about ten more minutes hammering at the keys, chugging down the rest of his energy drink. *Crap.* It was past noon and he had a needy woman to contend with.

Snatching another drink, he looked down into the rain. Washington, D.C. was a foreign place to him. A large city that left him trapped. He never felt lost however, because someone would find him. Something always plagued him though. Why was there no zombie outbreak in D.C.? One in fifty people abroad had turned, yet a much smaller fraction in the nation's capital was afflicted. No senators, congressmen, joint chiefs, or Supreme Court Justices crossed the undead path. The conspiracy theories should have abounded, but they did not. It was a theory that only a few others he knew still talked about.

He was tapping his finger on the side of the black and blue can. He had been digging and thought he found something worthwhile, but there was no one to tell. *I wonder what Henry will think.* Most of his friends and family were gone, and he never seemed to have time to make new ones. Henry Bawkula was about the only one he ever contacted over the years. Henry he could trust, but he knew his college friend wouldn't feel the same about him. *Not after Jeanine.*

He moved forward on his search, as every day he felt like something was about to happen, something big was going on. He was a liar, and he knew a liar when he heard one, and those who proclaimed him a hero were the worst liars by far. He used to lie to stay out of trouble, but they lied for power and he felt caught in the middle. He wanted to disappear.

He dragged himself over, slumped down in his cloth sectional and began playing the latest Darkslayer RPG game on his television screen. *Ah yes, my favorite escape from reality, smash-mouth fantasy.* He had spent over an hour chopping down monsters with a massive battle axe when the power went off. The overcast sky provided gray light in an otherwise black room. It was dead quiet, other than the beating rain. He stepped out of his study and looked down at the black furniture silhouettes in his living room. His knee began to ache again as he looked outside at the other buildings whose lights were still on.

A weird feeling overcame him. *What was that!?* Something shifted in the shadows, he was sure of it.

"Christy?" he whispered. There was no reply. "Christy?"

He waited on the landing, squinting. Fear filtered inside him as he stepped down the stairs. He began to relax as the edges of his furniture became clear, and he began to recognize the layout in the dim light.

He banged his knee on the edge of an antique buffet. *OW!*

He stubbed his toe on a couch leg. "Dammit!" His eyes began to water as he hobbled towards his bedroom.

He felt stupid as he sipped more fluid from his canister.

I don't even have a flashlight. Or match—Or candle—Stupid!

There never had been a need. He pushed the cracked bedroom door open. The heavy curtains had remained closed and the room was as black as a coal mine. He knew his way around and made it over to Christy's side. He ran his hand along the small of her back and caressed her hair. He shook her body a bit.

"Hey," he said softly.

She didn't respond.

"Hey!" he whispered in her ear. "Wake up!"

He ran his hand down her back, over her rump and up again. She didn't stir. He jostled her hair. Nothing happened. He felt something wet on his hand. He held it to his face.

What the hell is this? It was dark, sticky and warm. He shook her hard, panic coursing through him, but she didn't move.

"Christy! Christy! Wake up baby! Wake—ulp!"

Something seized him from behind, strangling his neck and squeezing his throat. He felt like a bear had a hold on him as he tried to scream, but his tongue did not move. *Help! Help! Dear God help me!* A sharp needle sunk deep into his neck, injecting a fluid that burned like fire. His body went numb as he felt himself fall helpless onto his bed.

CHAPTER 18

"**W**HAT HAPPENED!? WHAT HAPPENED!?"

Henry was almost yelling. The distraught look on her sweet face unsettled him. They had been going at it for over fifteen minutes. Sitting on the car hood, arms folded, she kept her head buried in her chest. He knew how stubborn she could be. They'd been on again, off again, over the years, and this was a big reason why. She wouldn't talk about some things to him. She stuffed things deep inside, unwilling to share her past. This was another one of those times.

He asked her again, cheeks reddening more by the second.

"Was it Jimmy? Did he say something perverted to you?"

She shook her head back and forth, choking at the sound of the name.

"Come on...tell me what is wrong, you're driving me crazy," he said, immediately wishing he had not let those words out.

"What!" she said, raising her voice and head, mascara running from her eyes.

"I'm driving you crazy!?" She slipped off the hood of her car.

Oh no, here we go. Henry stepped away.

"You leave me here—for two weeks—with these—perverts! Your sick bastard of a brother shows up and ogles me like a webcam slut... and you think I'm crazy!"

He was being driven further backward. Tori's fingernails poked into his chest as her voice echoed off the concrete walls of the garage. There was nothing he could do now. Stanley warned him about these Italian women, and it wasn't as cute as it used to be.

"I'm sorry," he said as he slipped on some gravel, shielding himself with his hands. He never would have thought worrying about the feelings of a woman would make him want to crawl in a hole. Moments like this made him miss being a bachelor. He wanted to know what was wrong however, so he stood his ground. He had to do something fast. In a quick gentle motion, he caught her up in his arms and squeezed.

"What are you doing—let go!" she demanded, trying to pound his chest.

He didn't though, holding her tight, hoping she wouldn't knee him in the gonads like she had done once before.

"Forgive me. You don't have to tell me anything."

His words softened her body and he could feel her pull close. Tori wrapped her arms behind his back. The smell of her exotic perfume, coupled by her warm body, aroused his senses. Things were beginning to feel better, as his and her longing were beginning to be intertwined by the rush of emotion and adrenaline. He wanted her now, and he felt she needed him. Her sobbing turned into low passionate whimpers as her hot lips pressed into his neck.

The sound of the garage elevator opening interrupted his thoughts and he pulled away. Someone was rushing his way. He pushed Tori behind him.

"Is everything okay?" It was Rudy. His chubby face was flushed red.

"What do you mean, *'is everything okay?'*" Henry asked.

"Well," the hairy man stopped to catch his breath, "...it was like you guys both disappeared. I've been trying to find you for the past twenty minutes."

"Did you call my cell phone?"

"Yes!" Rudy retorted, pointing at Henry's waist.

Reaching down, he realized his phone case was empty on his belt, and a quick pat down of his clothes revealed he was without the mobile device.

"Oh...sorry."

He wasn't embarrassed however. Tori was still hugging him tight from the side. Rudy was giving her a funny look.

"Hey, were you guys about to get busy," Rudy said, wiggling his hips.

"No!" she said.

Henry intervened, "She's just upset," he felt her arms tighten around his waist, "...that I've been gone so long." He did the best he could on the fly.

His friend was rubbing his messy beard.

"Ah...so you *weren't* getting busy. I get it." Rudy winked and said, "Brown chicken, brown cow."

Henry stood there gawking at his friend whose mind had wandered somewhere else. As the awkward moment passed, he asked again, "Now, why did you need to get a hold of me?"

Rudy seemed confused, as if he'd just woken up and finally said, "Uh..." his eyes lit up, "oh shit, that's right, Louie is missing man. Louie is frickin' missing!"

Tori let out a sharp gasp beside him. He couldn't believe his ears. It wasn't possible. There were security cameras everywhere and every precaution was taken. His thoughts went to Jimmy and another chill went down his spine.

"What!? What do you mean? He can't be missing! It's not possible—"

"Man, I'm telling you, he's gone. Me and Weege have been looking for almost an hour."

"An hour! Why didn't you tell me sooner?" he yelled, as he rushed back toward the elevator.

Idiots. All of them. Trusting Jimmy. He wanted to kill somebody as he hammered at the only button outside the elevator.

"Tori, you stay here," he shouted.

"Hell no, I'm going in."

He grabbed her, "No, you're going home."

She jerked away from him, "Don't tell me no Mister, I've got a job here, too." She glared at Rudy who turned away from her angry stare. "I'm sure it's not going to be that big a problem."

He'd rather face a zombie than her wrath again, so he let it go. "Where's Ralph? Is he looking?"

"No, he left an hour ago, sick as a dog. He puked something awful," Rudy said with a sour look on his face.

Henry didn't see Ralph's car. He looked up at the elevator light. It was red. He kicked the door.

"You got to use your card man, the button don't work," Rudy said scanning his card.

Nothing happened. Henry tried his and Tori hers. Nothing happened. Something wasn't right and he had to get in there. His dad and Weege were in certain danger. Henry, Rudy and Tori were, too.

CHAPTER 19

Washington, DC

EVERYTHING INSIDE OF NATE MCDANIEL was screaming for help. His life was rushing through his thoughts. Those last moments with Jeanine, good and bad, resurfaced more than anything. That's what they say happens when you're about to die. You think about what you loved most.

He knew there were at least two people in the room, one was the big one that had turned him over like a rag doll, the other he wasn't sure. The lights had come back on and he could hear thunder cracking in his ears. He couldn't move an inch. He could see his assailant better now, broad and ugly faced, flat nosed, a grin of yellowed teeth, wearing a tailored blue suit. The man's powerful hands clutched at his clothes, sitting him upright like a mannequin on the bed's edge.

His neck was sideways, looking at the

other figure. *You're the son of a bitch that shot Jeanine!* The same man stood in front of him, small, clad in black, a short moustache, and the dark countenance of a killer.

The little man's Southern accent was heavy as he spoke, "Well, asshole that saved the world...look what you done gone and got yourself into. You killed yer girlfriend and killed yerself."

WHAT!? Nate tried to shake his head, but couldn't.

The man's face was inches from his, and Nate could see his own watery eyes in the man's dark sunglasses. The man's breath was pure tobacco, and he could see the man's jutting lower lip.

"Now, why would the jackass that saved the world do something like that?"

He could feel his hair being pulled back as his head was being shaken for him. *I didn't kill anybody! I'm not killing myself! Please don't kill me!*

His head was let go as the little man stepped away and sat in a chair in front of him. He wanted to scream. He wanted to cry so bad, beg for his life or anything, but he couldn't do either.

His captor continued, "You see boy, you did save the world, and that pissed a lot of people off. I think you know who I'm talking about. You know that den of world leaders that patted you on the back and gave you a bunch of bullshit accommodations..."

Nate thought he blinked, but he wasn't sure.

"...Yep, you might look dumb, but I knew you weren't. I tried to tell them. We should have killed you the day we found you, but they needed someone to make them look good. Stupid politicians..."

What are you talking about? I didn't do anything! Oh God—please don't let him kill me!

"...and sure, rich jerkoffs like you get bored sometimes and start getting too nosey. The last thing we need, or the World Humanitarian Society rather, is the man who saved the world pronouncing conspiracy theories..."

The man was straddling the kitchen chair, as causal as if he'd been conversing with his best friend. He watched as the little man spit dark juice into his favorite coffee cup.

"You couldn't be happy, like a fattened calf, could ya boy. All the money, fame, glory and poontang couldn't satisfy your quest for why things happened. Things people don't give a shit about anymore. No—you had to lump yourself in with all the other nut cases out there, and figure out where the zombies came frum."

The man pinched his fingers almost together, inches from his face.

"You got this close," the man said in a dry hiss.

Nate could see the other, big man cross his path and begin moving something on the bed behind him. A bottle of something rattled near his ears. There were sirens somewhere, as well as other sounds intermingling with the heavy rain and rolling thunder.

What is happening? Dude, I don't know that much. I can't prove anything. Please don't kill me! You don't have to kill me!

He saw the seated man pull out a pistol, automatic and nickel plated. The gun looked like a shiny club in the man's small hand. He envisioned Jeanine's head blowing open like a bloody watermelon again. *Please not me! Please not me! Dear God, please not me!*

"Yeah boy, it's time to tie up the loose ends."

The small man stood up and pulled the slide on his weapon.

Shick–tick!

Nate could see the man twist a silencer onto the gun barrel as his adversary stepped out of sight. *Where is he! Where is he! I don't want to die like this.* He wondered what would happen after he died. He hoped the stories he heard as a boy about Jesus were true. He had nothing else to hope for. He remembered Jeanine's cross on his neck. *Jesus save me.* He didn't want to die. *Please forgive me for all the things I did and did not do.* He could feel his heart sinking.

Something cold was being pressed into his right hand. It was steel. His body was being turned around on the bed. He saw some pictures of friends and family on the dresser tops. There were pills he hadn't seen before there, too. There was white powder in a small bag by his mirror. He caught a good look at himself as his repositioners took a pause. The big man, missing some teeth, was grinning above him as Nate stared in the mirror. He was pasty, slack-jawed and pathetic. His pupils were wide and glossy, like a zombie. The wiry Southerner stuck another needle in his arm.

"This is so they think you took all those drugs we scattered about."

There was a slapping on his shoulder as they panned him around. A gold plated can of Mountain Dew was on his night stand. *All this, over that!* He was facing his pillowed headboard now. He saw Christy's frozen stare. A thick patch of blood soaked the sheets behind her back. His arm was raised before him, a gun inside his grasp. *No! Please no! How can you be so cruel! This can't be real! I didn't do anything! I saved the world!*

"Be thankful Son, you could have died a zombie. Heh. Heh."

CHAPTER 20

Guthrie, WV

HIS INVINCIBILITY COMPLEX HAD TAKEN over. Every devious plan had worked so far. Spinning around in the security desk chair, Jimmy shouted at the top of his lungs.

"I'm the next Nate McDaniel! I'm the King! The world is mine!" He let out a high pitched *'WOOOOOO'* like a rock star.

The monitors provided humorous activity as he watched his brother pound on the elevator door inside the garage. *Thinks he's so smart. We'll see.* His stepfather Stanley, still in the basement lab, was oblivious to the chaos as he attempted to waltz with Jimmy's undead mother. *Scratch him mom! Bite him!* He hated Stanley as much as the rest, but mainly because of his brother. His stepfather had always been good to him. They'd had good times fishing and playing ball, but he didn't remember those days anymore.

Jimmy was now consumed with the bankroll he would get when he turned over the XT Serum. But that wouldn't happen until his secret employers had some proof it worked. That was where Louie came in.

Jimmy started laughing as he watched Weege pulling at the thick mop of black hair on his head, screaming at the monitors

Tsk–Tsk, Weege! You should have paid closer attention. Instead, the frail little geek from Dubai chose to jam on his smart phone, play games, and come to the aid of his ailing counterpart Ronald. Ronald was a cautious master of many things, except his diet. *The world's greatest Big Chug fan, down at last.* Squeezing eye drops into Ronald's drink had sent the man running to the toilet and then all the way home.

His mind seemed to grasp the entire understanding of the universe as he sucked down another can of light beer. Crushing it in his hands, he cut himself.

"Damn!"

He laughed like a hyena. It had all been so easy. Ronald's leaving allowed him to shut down the elevator, just long enough to switch Louie into another cell. Weege never suspected he had run a separate loop over his security feed, until it was too late. Meanwhile, the zombie boy was safe in an adjacent cell they thought was empty, because of another bogus video feed. Rudy was too lazy to physically go and check, relying on the video cameras instead. Jimmy orchestrated all of this from inside the small security room.

He watched the zombie boy Louie on another screen. The boy was wound up like a kitten, ready to pounce on a ball of yarn. The hefty gray boy circled his cell at alarming speed. *He looks like Frankenstein on crack.* Jimmy giggled to himself. Now there was only one more thing left to do. Let the little monster loose. He checked the screen monitoring the garage. *You ready, brother big shot. How about you, stupid slut and sloppy boy?* He hated them all. He couldn't wait to see them suffer. Still, he wanted to savor it.

The sound of Metal Maiden's song, 'Run from the Hills', began playing inside his pocket, causing him to lurch. He got out his phone, dropped it, cursed, and then answered it.

"Hello," he said, in a voice as dull as a spoon. He snorted heavily, his glassy eyes intent on the words coming from another side.

"The live feed is down JB 111. We need to see some data. A storm's hitting your area, so the boss wants it all done now. Execute the plan. Get the data on tapes. Lock it down and get the serum. No one leaves alive but you."

He felt cold for a moment, shifting in his

seat. He swallowed hard as he said, "Uh...yes sir. Uh...did you say no one?"

"That's right boy. You want to save the world—you got to make some choices. Can you do it?

The voice on the other end was harsh, unfamiliar, maybe foreign, he couldn't tell.

"Yes...Yes sir."

"Good, Son. Execute within the hour."
Click

He saw all of their faces on the screens again and swallowed. He didn't want them all to go, just two.

They don't like me. They judge me. All of them. Screw em' all. Now it's my time.

The hard surfaces in the security room closed in on him, and he felt surrounded by darkness. He snorted heavily again and snorted in another white line.

I can do this. I'm gonna be the next Nate McDaniel.

He typed away at his computer, and watched as the elevator opened in the parking garage. The stunned group stepped inside, but not before Henry looked back at the garage camera. He could swear his brother could see him. *Screw you Henry!*

CHAPTER 21

THE TRIP BACK THROUGH THE hallways and sliding steel doors was agonizing. *Red. Green. Red. Green.* A wild zombie was on the loose, and fear festered inside all of their bellies as they passed from room to room. Henry had no idea what to expect. Rudy stepped on the backs of his heels again. He shoved the man in front of him. His concerns for his father were heavy, and as far as he understood his friend's blathering, Stanley didn't know. He had a shotgun now, but no ammo. *Jimmy.* Shells were in short supply, but there were always some in the weapons locker.

'We Got the Heat' began ringing on Rudy's phone as they stood in the secure corridor just outside of the zombie playroom.

"It's Weege," Rudy said, "What's going on man? Did you find the little zombie turd yet?"

He held the phone up, speaker on. Weege's

foreign dialect was crystal clear and full of excitement.

"I got him! He's in another cell!"

They all looked at one another in relief, except Henry.

"How'd he get in another cell Weege?"

"I don't know. My computer froze up, and I noticed I was on a repeating video feed. It had to be Jimmy screwing around again. Just like the last time. He's — a — bastard!"

That Jimmy was. The last time he forgot to feed the zombies and two people almost died. Jimmy said it was an accident, but Henry knew it wasn't. Maybe it was drugs, maybe it was intentional, but it was time for Jimmy to go.

"Weege, its Henry, are you sure that Louie is locked up?"

"Yes, I can see it on the screen. He's a busy little monkey, but he isn't going anywhere."

He could feel Tori's nails digging into his side.

"Have you checked the cages?"

There was a pause. "No — I'm not going down there."

"Why not? We have to be sure."

"You go. It's not in my job description."

Rudy butted in and said, "You're a stand up guy Weege."

"I'm alive. I'm staying alive like disco, Baby. This episode is freaking me out. I can't believe what happened today!"

The sound in Weege's voice seemed to allude to something else, but Henry wasn't sure.

"What do you mean?"

"A...just come up here. You need to see for yourself."

"Why?" Tori said.

"It's better that way."

Tori scanned her security pass and the door slid open. A zombie was standing nearby and she let out a screech. The small child didn't notice, as it shuffled back in the rainbow room mumbling 'num-num'. Henry took a quick head count and saw all the children except Louie. *All here, good.* The vivid colors, cartoon screens and classical music were amplified, making him feel like he was inside a carnival's madhouse. They crept inside, wary of the zombie children whose sunken faces stared on and past them like shadows.

Climbing up the ladder tubes, Rudy had the pleasure of going up last, tongue hanging out like a wild man, behind Tori. She hadn't noticed.

"Mother of mercy," he muttered underneath her high heels.

Traipsing over the catwalks, they converged on Weege's station. The excited man was in his thirties, with big brown eyes and a teenager's face and build. A thin goatee patch was under his chin. He was sweating and motioning for them to come closer.

"Look! Look! Look!" he cried, pointing to his computer screen.

Henry expected to see a zombie doing cartwheels, but it wasn't what he expected at all. It was an Internet news site headline. His heart sank as he read it. "Man Who Saved the World Found Dead! Murder! Suicide!" He murmured over the details.

"Nate McDaniel was found dead inside his D.C. condominium at 12:45 EST today. Inside sources say that Christy Backwater from FNN News was found dead inside the penthouse as well. A pistol and casings were found at Mr. McDaniel's bedside. The two had last been seen leaving together from her TV studio. The nature of the relationship was not known, but the evidence of drugs, including sex enhancing stimulants, suggests an elitist bootie call gone bad."

Henry finished the rest to himself. He could feel Tori hugging and sobbing at his side and Rudy patting his back. They didn't know Nate. But he knew this couldn't have happened like the news said. His old friend was too smart for that. He looked up and saw Weege pointing a smart phone his way. "What are you doing?"

"I wanted to capture the look on your faces

when you saw the news. Very interesting. See — look!"

He held out the picture of their frozen expressions: mouths wide, brows high and shock growing on each face.

"Why don't you make a poster too, Moron," Tori said. "I'm sorry, Baby," she said, rubbing Henry's back.

He hadn't heard from Nate in months, other than the occasional text. He never understood what Nate McDaniel went through, but he felt worse than he ever would have imagined somehow. All of Nate's interviews were disingenuous as far as he was concerned. It all had to be scripted. Maybe he had more to say and someone stopped it.

"Man, Christy Backwater is dead? She was hot! That's terrible man." Rudy was sitting down and watching live news casts while munching on Weege's nacho cheese chips. "Best legs I'd ever seen."

Tori smacked him in the head.

"Not better than yours...of course...Tori."

"She's dead idiot — show some respect!"

"Sorry."

Henry sat down at another station, and his face was lined with concern and wonder. He hated this place, the zombies and everything. The most popular man in the world was dead. He needed to tell his dad. *Crap.* What about

Jimmy and Louie? He'd forgotten all about that.

"Where's my phone? Where's my phone?" He looked at his friends, who were now crammed around Weege's monitor, fighting for position. Henry headed to his station and there it was, setting on the desk. A few new text messages were there. *Tori. Tori. Tori. Nate 1215?* Opening it he saw the following letters: CPWWSZH.

It didn't make any sense, but he knew it was a warning. Jumbles were something they played in college, each trying to top the other. They also used it for other things. It was their own language they created for themselves and some others. If it was indeed serious, he knew he might be in danger.

"What is it, Lover?" Tori said in his ear.

He looked at her saying, "I got a message from Nate this morning. It might be a warning. It might be why he was killed." He didn't know why he was telling her this, but now didn't seem like a time for secrets. Too many changes in the status quo were abounding around him. His mind raced to lock it down. This couldn't all be randomly happening on the same day. There had to be a reason.

Her voice was excited, "What does it say?"

He showed her the phone.

"What does that mean?"

"I don't know yet, but I'll figure it out."

"Let's ask Weege, he might know — he's a freak like that."

He was firm as he pulled her back saying, "No—keep this between us, Tori. I'll get it. I need them to focus on the next step."

He could see concern growing on her sweet face. He knew she trusted him and would do anything for him, but her tongue slipped from time to time.

"What is the next step?" she whispered.

"It's time to lock up the zombies. There has been a breach and I need to tell Dad."

"Just call him."

"We tried." Rudy had sauntered over. "You know he won't answer. He never does. As for the breech, he won't report it. He's too afraid they'll shut us down."

He spoke up, "Okay, Weege get over here." They all gathered. "Let's lock up the rest of the zombies. We need to gather Dad and Jimmy. I have a bad feeling this place isn't safe. I'm going to check on Louie. Weege, monitor the floors..."

Henry looked around.

"Is anyone else here?"

"It's after five, Dude, the rest have rolled, it's just the night shift," Rudy said.

"Okay then, you and Tori go down there and latch the cages."

His friends gave him a funny look.

"Okay, I'll go with you. You don't know

how to lock them without the security cards. I'll show you. Let's go."

Their footfalls rushed over the platform, across the catwalk and down the ladders. He hated this. Herding the zombies was dangerous because they were stubborn. This was what he needed Ronald for. The burly man would bundle up, round up the children and toss them in. It wasn't something the rest of them usually had to do.

A simple scratch from a zombie would garner a feverish reaction, but their bites were fatal. There wasn't anything you could do. He could see the worry on their faces as they donned heavy cotton beige suits and thick padded gloves. There were over a dozen cells along the outer wall, like ones you would see in an animal shelter, but much larger and secure. Tori opened up several of them, side by side. Each hatch had a red light.

Here we go. "You ready Rudy?"

"Yeh, who are we getting first?"

"Peggy. She's the easiest."

They surrounded a gaunt little girl who was dressed in a Halloween outfit and appeared to be about five years old. The child stood before a large flat screen television that showed nerdy little kids singing and playing instruments.

"On three, Rudy!" he shouted through a mesh-faced protective mask. His heart was pounding. He'd never done this before. "One... Two...Three!"

Each man locked his hands around the girl's wrists and stretched her arms taunt. He could feel her little arms pulling back, strong like a small animal, but not strong enough. Her fingers clutched as they dragged her toward the cell, but she wasn't fighting. They had her inside, let her go, and each rushed back out. Tori scanned the door lock. It turned from red to green. Henry was relieved.

"Here's how you do the double lock," he said with a muffled voice.

There was a small concealed handle at the top of the silver cage, like one used to open or close an old window. He spun it around until it clicked.

"You got it Gorgeous!" Tori said.

"I got it Baby!" he winked inside his mask.

"I'm sweating my ass off and I'm still single. Can we get this over with, you two love turds!" Rudy exclaimed.

"Okay Rudy, okay. Tori, be sure to double lock those other cages too, we don't want the rest accidentally getting out."

One by one, using the same tactic, they got the other zombie kids inside. The zombies resisted with only the chronic 'Num-Num' phrase. Oh, to have a muzzle on them, Henry thought. He'd do anything to never hear those words again. It took about thirty minutes with little Mike, because he wouldn't let go of the jungle gym. The little boy in Quantum Leap pajamas, provided by Rudy, had been clutching the yellow-coated play set for hours. Henry considered cutting off the boy's fingers, but a screwdriver managed to pry them off.

"Ah...that sucked," he said, as they all took off their masks and anti-zombie suits.

Everyone's hair was matted and wet. Rudy was soaked head-to-toe in sweat, but the sight of Tori in damp jeans and a V-neck T-shirt made him sweat more. It made both men gawk. Her eyes enlarged when she looked their way and she made a dash for her lab coat.

"Man, you are one lucky dude. She is smoking."

The comment didn't bother him as it felt good for a change, having a woman like that.

"Hey! Hey guys!" It was Weege shouting from above in alarm. "Hey!"

They all walked over and looked up at him. Weege's dark face was ashen.

Henry yelled up, a smile on his face, "What is it Weege? Did the Pope die too?"

"No! No! It's Louie! He's gone again!"

CHAPTER 22

"**N**ATE MCDANIEL IS DEAD?" JIMMY said, as a hysterical laugh burst from his lips. He never would have known if he hadn't been watching all the commotion at Weege's station. Looks of alarm and surprise caught his fancy as he zoomed in another camera to see more. He watched from above the scene. The expressions on their faces excited his flesh. Their suffering brought him joy. He knew his time had come, and it was his turn to be the most famous man in the world.

He checked his recordings on the screens from the security room, and they were all in order. The monitors were saving every image and clip for his purpose. He knew the live feed might go. It happened from time-to-time, and that is why he made a backup recording. The remote area created havoc on communications when the wind and rain came. He could see his stepfather Stanley singing to the undead girls inside the biolab. As far as he could tell, they weren't going anywhere.

Jimmy rubbed his nose, snorted, and looked for his brother Henry. *Go ahead brain child. Go put up the zombies. I've got a surprise for you.*

He Googled Nate McDaniel's and Christy Backwater's faces on his smart phone. He touched her face on the screen. "Oh yeah, babes like you will soon be mine."

He finished off another can of beer and pulled up the action in Louie's cell. He bit his dirty fingernails while twisting his ball cap around before he entered a code. His foot was tapping as he waited. Jimmy had not only helped Stanley give Louie the XT Serum, but he also had been starving the boy. The lack of zombie dew that kept the children docile would build Louie's hunger for flesh and brains. He saw to it Louie missed his doses. The XT serum sped up the boy's metabolism as well as other things. That's what his employers told him to do. That is what he did.

Jimmy looked at another camera feed; he could see them in the zombie suits, jerking the little minions into their holes. He loved doing that. He hated the rotten little fiends. His life could have been perfect if not for them. They took his life, his friends and family in a single day, all but Henry and Stanley, the ones he despised most. It was then that the world of madness consumed him and crushed his soul. He couldn't cope with all the changes. He survived the only way he could, like a rodent that feeds off others. He considered suicide, but he didn't want to leave this miserable world for the next. Those were his thoughts back when, but he didn't remember them anymore, as many memories were a clump of fried brain cells. He just wanted to feel great all the time. He wanted to be the next Nate McDaniel.

He could see them in the kiddy zoo now, and he knew they were talking about him. *Stop talking about me. I might show mercy.* He pressed RETURN on the keyboard.

"Bye-bye douche bags!"

CHAPTER 23

A FAMILIAR SOUND FILLED HIS HEAD. He turned to face it. An opening stood before him and he couldn't help but pass through. Many colors and objects were beside him, behind him and below him. Everything was spinning, moving and stopping. There was blackness, and there was the light. Something was shuffling below him and humming above him. He heard sounds before him and said, "Numma–Numma."

Louie didn't understand where he was or what he was doing. He ran his hands over the cold metal walls of the day care. He could hear voices, but he didn't understand. He smelled things, but didn't know what that meant. He needed something, but he didn't know what it was. He had to find it. Everything was blurry though. The shapes seemed to make sense, but the spectrum of bright colors annoyed him. Somewhere nearby was what he needed. Instinct pressed him that way, as more objects rushed past him. The sounds of voices became louder, and he stopped moving. The hunger was building inside of him as he moved toward the sound. It was food he wanted, and it was near. He just didn't know what the food was.

Louie didn't know what the loud words meant, but they frightened him.

Someone shouted, "Sound the alarm Weege!"

CHAPTER 24

IT HAD BEEN ONE OF those days that lasted a lot longer than normal. The midday sun had long passed and the dark clouds above were filled with rolling thunder. The heavy breeze was such that John had closed the guard shack door. His feet ached from all the standing and his butt was sore from all the sitting. Over an hour had gone by without a word between him and his grandson. The boy was intent with his video games, and not much for conversation.

"Is that battery ever gonna die Fergie?

The boy looked up, rubbing his puffy brown eyes and said, "I've got more batteries. There's a plug-in here too."

"Oh...Wanna play some cards?'

"No."

Shrugging, John pulled a card deck out from a top desk drawer. The guard shack was accommodating. It had an air conditioner filled with icy air and a toasty heater as well.

A back-up diesel generator was outside, but he had never used it. There was a beige push button phone sitting on the counter, but it only made calls inside the facility. He had never used it before, either, and didn't know anyone who had.

He dealt out a hand of solitaire with his blue and white drugstore cards. He hadn't won in weeks, but maybe this would be his lucky day...but he didn't feel lucky. He felt like a man in the forest tracking a bear, waiting for the big beast to show up at any second. He wiped the dampness from his forehead. *Why am I sweating?*

Sprinkles of rain came and went with an occasional rumble of thunder. Somewhere in the distance he swore he heard a tree fall.

"Hey Fergie, why don't you help me out with these cards? You were always good at this."

The boy looked up, his freckled cheeks smudged with snack cake fudge.

Messy boy.

The boy replied, "Do I have to? I'm comfortable."

He sighed, "Suit yourself."

After a couple of rounds of solitaire passed with failure, he shuffled the deck again and dealt a new set on the counter. He kept thinking about what a long day it had been, as he looked outside, stroking his moustache.

His stomach was growling. He opened the

door and inhaled some fresh air. The cold drizzle was refreshing on his face. The facility was quiet as always. He hoped someone would come out. It had been a while since Ronald left without having said a word, green as a toad. *Poor fella, never seen him look worse and he looks bad enough to begin with.*

Taking his glasses off, he squinted at the facility. The green lights spread on the fence posts had turned red. About then, a fierce wind picked up forcing him back inside, and he closed the door with a loud smack, causing the boy to lurch from his seat.

"Ferguson, did you see those lights turn red?"

"Uh-huh."

"Well, how long ago did that happen?"

There was a pause.

"Fergie! How long?" he almost shouted, as a chill rushed through his veins.

The boy took the time to check his watch and said, "Maybe forty minutes."

John felt all of his muscles tighten between his shoulder blades, "Forty minutes!"

He didn't know what to do. Those lights had never come on before. He grabbed the telephone. It rang, and kept ringing. He left it off the hook. A sudden gust rocked the shack and the wind began to howl like banshees.

The boy had a stunned look, and fear in his eyes. The boy dropped his game as he cried out, "Grandpa!"

John rushed over and put his arms around the boy. The child was shaking and clutching at his clothes.

"Come on Fergie, let's get in the truck." The boy didn't want to go anywhere, not letting go of his legs. The wind was so loud he couldn't hear his own voice. He tried to pick the boy up.

"Fergie, let me go!" he hollered.

He was nervous now, feeling trapped inside the shack as the heavy rain began beating down on the metal roof like rocks. If he didn't get moving, they might be in for a long night. It hurt him to do so as he hoisted the boy up into his arms, tearing the muscles in his aged back. Somehow, he slung a hundred pounds of dead weight over his shoulder and stepped into the unexpected maelstrom.

The rain soaked him the second he stepped outside, splashing him like a thousand tiny waves. The winds were roaring in his ears, and he could see where a large pine had fallen onto the fence. He fought through the wind and could hear the boy's terrified screams in his ears. He forced his way through the chaos and fumbled for the handle on his truck door. He opened it and blockaded himself inside the door as the boy crawled inside like a frightened rabbit. He jumped inside the cabin as the wind slammed the door behind him.

"Sweet Mary!" he said, wiping off his

soaked face with his hand. "Where did that come from?"

"Take me home Grandpa! Take me home!" the boy urged, crawling under the glove box.

He was going to do just that, but he hesitated. The sheets of rain came, and he could see the red lights flickering against the facility. He figured they would need help, but he wasn't going in, he'd just make a call from down the road. He didn't want to leave anyone hanging, either. What if they needed help? A blinding flash dazzled his vision as lightning struck the ground between the fence and the facility. It scared him to death. The boy was screaming.

"We're going boy! We're gone!"

He fired the big white truck up with a roar as classic country blared from the speakers. He couldn't see much of anything, but he knew the road. He backed up, fish tailing the truck around and taking off. He didn't get too carried away moving down the road, but in his rear-view mirror he thought he saw a tree fall on his guard shack. *That was too close!* Every harrowing minute he felt safer the further he went. The storm seemed to worsen as he winded down the hill. He stopped the truck.

"Grandpa, what are you doing?"

He wanted to go back; it was the right thing to do. He grabbed his grandson's shaking leg, and gave the situation serious thought. It came down to a choice between life or death. *Get Fergie home or his grandma will kill me.*

"Screw that mess!" he said as he jumped on the gas.

"Grandpa..."

"Yes Fergie?"

"I don't want to work with you anymore," the boy said as they headed down the hill.

"That's okay, can't say I'd blame you."

He was worried about the people inside. They should be safe, but he would probably be fired for leaving. If there were zombies in there, he hoped they didn't make it out. He'd have to let somebody know, but it would have to wait. He was going home. Family comes first.

The roads were covered with rising water when he reached the bottom of the hill and turned on the main road. A wave of water on the windshield that was followed by another giant splash blinded his sight. A small convoy of black vans and SUV's raced past him, the likes he had not seen in a long time. He couldn't say for sure, but he had a pretty good guess where they were headed. *That's odd.* Maybe those folks inside didn't need his help after all. Maybe things were worse than he imagined. Maybe he was wrong. He muttered a prayer.

CHAPTER 25

INSIDE THE FACILITY, THE LIGHTS were flickering like humming bird wings, sending shivers of fear down everyone's spine. In the back of his mind, Henry fully expected the hyperactive zombie child to charge from underneath a pile of toys at any moment. He spun slowly around, with his head on a swivel, as his friends did the same.

"Where is he Weege!?" he yelled.

A frantic figure raced over the catwalk and leaned over the guard rail aghast.

"I don't know, he could be anywhere? Hurry—get up here."

Rudy and Tori looked over at him with frightened eyes.

"Go up there and help him, I have to tell Dad and find Jimmy."

She grabbed his arm.

"You have to come up—until we find him! He has to be in here, there's nowhere he can go." Her voice was shaking, and her hand trembled as she said it. "This is bad, I can feel it. We have to stick together. Don't go!" she urged.

He took her in his arms, and he didn't want to go anywhere. He was torn. If something happened to his brother he could live with that, but not his step dad. No, Stanley wouldn't be ready for the unexpected.

"I've got to go. I love you!"

He gave her a long hard kiss. He could feel her warm tears on his cheek, and when he looked back in her eyes he could see how frightened she was. He didn't want to leave her.

"Now get up there you two!"

Rudy was already up the ladder shoot as he pushed her along. She went up with heavy sobs. He ran over to the cages and checked that all of the children were secured. Each quick glance confirmed they were safe.

The playroom was a long oval, almost four thousand square feet. The cages ran along the back walls of the odd arcna. One of those cages should have housed Louie, and it was on the other side.

He put on his suit and mask, then took the mask back off. It blocked too much of his peripheral vision. *This suit better work.* He passed by the locked cages, expecting something to lunge at him any second. Another shotgun was racked along the wall; he pulled it off and checked the chamber. It was empty and the ammo box was nowhere to be found. He pulled one shell from his lab coat pocket. It was buckshot, a joke from John the guard long ago. The old man told him it would bring him luck. But would it kill a zombie? *Better than nothing.*

He moved fast along the inner perimeter until he approached cage 17, where Louie was last seen. He stopped, loaded the shotgun, and leveled it at his hips. *Here we go.* He was burning up inside, sweat soaking his suit inside and out.

He jumped in front of the cage door, but nothing was there. He felt relief, but only for a moment. He had begun to back toward the center of the room when he noticed something. The light to the security room door was green. It was open, just enough for a boy to squeeze through. *Crap.* He could see white light spilling from the crack, and he knew what he had to do. He hoped he would find a trapped zombie in there.

He scanned his badge and a negative beep sounded, so he peeked inside. The florescent lights inside were flickering, causing a strobe effect. He was sure nothing was in there, but at the other end the elevator was open, like the mouth of a black tunnel. A red light glimmered above the entrance. He sucked in his breath, squeezed between the doors, wedging himself in between them. He was halfway through when the light turned red. *Oh no!* He was stuck. He felt a sharp pain as the door pinched his shoulder. The pressure was building. If Louie showed up now, it was over; he was trapped. Was this something Jimmy had done? Was his brother capable of murder? He pushed on the edge of the door, but it wouldn't give.

With a grunt of desperate determination, he pushed with all of his might. The door budged enough for him to force his body through. He flexed his shoulder. It wasn't dislocated, but it felt like it. He found little relief when he realized he was alone in the corridor. He noticed the light above the door was green again and the crack was still there. It was odd.

He headed toward the elevator shaft. *What am I going to do?* Step-by-step, he walked toward the elevator, shotgun ready. The closer he got, the more he could see of the dim outline of the elevator. The flickering lights made him feel like there was movement all around him. His heart was beating in his ears. Within ten feet the image inside became more clear. He stepped inside. The elevator was empty.

The buttons inside weren't lit as he pressed them a dozen times. It didn't make sense to him. There was power in the building, and the generators would be humming if there weren't, but he didn't hear them, and he usually could tell the difference. He started to worry. What if the power went out? They had been through storms before, but not with a zombie on the loose. What if lightning struck a generator or a tree fell on it? Everything was going wrong today, and dread sunk in deeper. Where was Louie? Where was Jimmy, and what about Stanley? Second thoughts surged in his mind; they should have stayed together. *Tori was right. I better head back.*

As he made his way back to the cracked door, he heard a blood curdling scream coming from the other side. It was Tori. He ran for the opening, but the door slid closed and the light turned red.

"NOOOOOO!" he screamed, but nobody heard.

CHAPTER 26

BETWEEN HEAVY SNORTS WERE JOSTLING flinches as the thunder rattled his core. The monitors were clear before him as he had arranged backup power. Jimmy was smarter than everybody and he knew it. He felt like the demi-god of a black dungeon, with the lives of others balancing on his whims. Now he was distracted, trying to reconnect the encrypted live feed to his associates. The live feed was still broken by the storm. It wasn't going to happen, so he had to resort to plan C, for he had forgotten B, and A was fading in his memory.

Now, enthralled with his own power, he turned Louie loose to feast on his former friends. He felt the excitement, like the first time he was in a brothel, when he saw the looks on their distraught faces. He watched as his brother was wiping sweat from his brow, agonizing over what to do next. He was laughing as if he hosted a horror film festival, fingers clasped together under his chin.

"Henry the zombie. Henry the zombie," he repeated in a childish tune. "Oh Henry, I am sorry I have to blow your head off! But this is how I save the world!"

He couldn't help himself; it was all coming together so well.

There was another problem, and paranoia set in as he remembered he had to get his stepfather's serum. The data he needed wasn't on the main server. No, his stepfather was too old fashioned. It was on Stanley's non-networked computer, at an isolated work station, pass-code protected and all. He had to get that data. Stanley wasn't going anywhere. His movements suggested there was nothing to worry about.

"Good Stan, just keep working like a fool."

Tori and Rudy were climbing the stair chutes like frightened chickens while Henry played the hero with an unloaded shotgun. *What an idiot!* Checking his monitors, Jimmy tried to locate Louie, dying to see the boy take a bite out of any of them, allowing him to record the show.

"Ah, there you are, Chunky."

There was an unlit alcove they used for storing many stuffed toys and other cuddly things. The boy was hunched over, pulling the stuffing from the inside of a massive light blue teddy bear. Louie was in husky jeans, tennis shoes and a blue striped shirt. The boy's brown hair was hanging down over half his face, while his chubby hands jammed white clumps of synthetic material in his mouth.

"You're eating the wrong thing, Stupid!" Jimmy shouted, poking the computer screen.

He watched a little longer, until his brother's movements caught his eye. Maybe his brother did have shotgun shells after all? Maybe Jimmy had missed some of them? He was certain he got them all. Or had he? Even so, he knew he could outsmart his brother. He cackled again.

Accessing the security and elevator door systems, he cracked open the main entrance to the romper room. His knees were bouncing up and down as he sat biting his nails. He watched with jovial clarity, zooming in on his brother's stern expression.

"Come on. Come on little wabbit."

His brother peered through the door and began to inch through. He hit a key, closing the door.

Jimmy jumped up with elation,

"Yes! I got you—you bastard!"

He couldn't believe it had been so easy. They were hamsters in his cage, and he ruled their world. A loud crash of thunder shook his bones, followed by a brilliant flash of white on the monitors, causing him to drop his beer can.

"Dammit!"

He looked at the outside monitors, but the wind and rain blocked his view of anything worth noticing. He had to get moving. He looked back at the screen and watched Henry force himself through.

"What!?"

His trap had failed, but that was temporary.

He followed his brother's movements, heading towards and away from the elevator. As Henry made his way back to the playroom, Jimmy saw something else happening. He closed the door just in time to see his running brother scream. There was another crack of thunder. Jimmy realized he couldn't watch. He had to get moving.

He stood inside the security room, which worked as a panic room of sorts. Inside it, he could safely execute his wicked intentions without anyone knowing. It used to be that three guards monitored the facility at all times, but now there was only one, lying on the floor dead as a stone. The guard was laughing and joking with Jimmy one moment, and shot with a taser the next. He hadn't moved since. The old man with crystal blue eyes and invigorating stories couldn't handle the final thrill. His heart gave out. Jimmy, as shocked as he was, laughed like a hyena at the thought. Now he bent down and took the dead fellow's .357 magnum. *This looks easy enough.* He aimed the gun at the old guard's head, pulled the trigger, and moved on.

The security room was in the basement, isolated like a bunker in the ground. A corridor went left and right as he exited. The left took him to the main elevator down to Stanley's lab. On the right was an emergency exit door, rarely used, and unknown to most. It was there he would make his glorious exit. He walked down the hall to the small lobby by the elevator, took the spiral stairs down, turned up the adjacent corridor and entered his stepfather's lab.

"Working hard Stan?" he said.

Stan looked up with worry and surprise on his face.

"Uh...yeah Son, you know me, I'm always working hard." His stepfather stood up tall and walked toward him. "I've been meaning to talk to you anyway, I'm glad you're here," Stanley said with his usual warm smile.

It took Jimmy off guard, and he slackened his grip on the pistol hidden inside the back of his pants. He saw his mother wandering toward him, bringing a sour look on his face.

"Let me guess, you and Mom are having a baby?"

Stanley's face darkened, and his tone

changed from a gentle creek to a crashing wave.

"You need to show some respect you little —"

"Little what, Pops?"

"I've done all I can for you, but even my patience is limited. You can say what you want to me, or about me," Stanley was towering over him, making him cringe, "but don't talk about your mother like that. Dead or alive!"

Jimmy wanted to crawl in a hole at that moment and began to have second thoughts. *What am I doing? What do I do? Why am I here?* Something reminded him of Nate McDaniel. *Oh yeah!* The evil twinkle in his eye returned, as fast as it had left, and Stanley stepped back with a look of uncertainty.

"Oh, I agree Stan," his voice was like a slithering snake as he snorted, wiping his nose on his sleeve. "As a matter of fact, I was just coming down to say good-bye. I have another job lined up. What do you think about that?"

Stanley was backing away as he spoke, looking for something.

"Oh...well that's great Son."

"I need a favor though," he said, stepping toward the autopsy table and glancing at the twins with a seedy smirk. "I need a reference."

"Sure Son, anything, let me type you up a letter."

"Great Stan, and while you are doing that,

whip me up all the paperwork for the XT Serum, I'll be needing that too."

Stanley turned as if someone had just been shot only to see the barrel of a gun lowered at his belly.

"N-N-Now—put that away, J-J-Jimmy."

Jimmy took a step forward saying, "Don't you mean 'Son'?"

"S-s-son."

"Give me the serum or I'll put you away—and don't call me Son!" he said, placing his other hand on the gun and pulling back the hammer with a click.

Stanley fidgeted in front of him, eyes fearful and darting.

"What do you want Son—excuse me—Jimmy?"

"Fire up that computer—put it all on here and give me the serum," he said, pulling out a jump drive. Stanley didn't move. Jimmy knew that Stanley kept all of the information on his own personal computer.

"Now!"

Stanley flinched and sat in defeat before his computer. Sweat was rolling down his crinkled forehead as he wiped his mouth and tried to log in. The shaking was so bad Stanley had trouble finding the keys.

"Hurry up!" he screamed into Stanley's ear.

Stanley held his hands up and said, "Okay,

I'm in. Here it is." Stanley looked back over his shoulder and shrugged.

"Load it on here."

"Come on Jimmy, don't do this. It's for all of us. That's why I brought you back," the man stood up, "...to celebrate."

He wanted to believe. He knew Stanley didn't lie. Stanley had been good to him. Something jostled him from behind.

BANG!

Jimmy screamed. He had squeezed the trigger as his mom's cold hands gripped his head and neck. He tore away, dropping the gun to the floor and running away. He saw his mother standing there, listless, with his hat and some hair in her hand. Stanley was kneeling before her, grasping his bloody belly, eyes filled with shock.

"Dad!" he cried, but he didn't know what to do.

He watched as Stanley clutched the waist of his late wife and looked up into her gaunt face.

Stanley was saying, "Though I walk in the shadow of the valley of death I shall fear no..." He died there, hands sliding down her legs, as her hand came down and stroked his head before she walked away.

Jimmy stood huffing in the corner, bewildered. It took almost a minute before he was able to move. Slowly, the power of greed gave him the strength to move. Stepping over his stepfather, he downloaded all of the files from that workstation as he snatched the jump drive. He slid open the glass doors of the refrigerator. Two glass bottles with cork tops were almost filled with a milky blue liquid marked XT. He found a black traveling case nearby with a syringe and needles stuffed in black foam inserts. Empty gaps were cut out the size of the bottles and he placed the serums inside, snapping the case closed. He checked his pocket and felt the jump drive. Now he had the serum in hand. He was worried as he looked around when he saw the gun laying on the floor by Stan. He snatched it up. He had it all.

"Yes!"

He looked over and saw his mom bumping between the autopsy tables.

"Bye Mom, next time I come back I'll have the cure."

Now it was time for him to finish off the rest.

CHAPTER 27

THEY WERE ALL TRANSFIXED AT their individual workstations above the daycare room. Everything was quiet as they clicked back and forth, trying to find images of the floor below them. Tori was more pressed to keep tabs on Henry. *Where is he? What's wrong?* Her monitor didn't show anything, just the same picture of the play room below, free of lumbering children. She wasn't the smartest girl in town, but she understood how to operate a computer. What twenty something didn't know how to these days? It was a second language if anything.

"You guys find anything?" she said, her voice trembling. She was picking at her lips between clicks on her mouse.

Rudy and Weege both answered, "No!"

Rudy added, "I don't know about you, but I don't think Louie is in there."

"He has to be! Find him or *you're* going down there," she said, shaking her fist.

"I'm not online! I don't have Internet!" a shrill voice said, like the sky was falling. The computers and cameras had been screwy ever since they got back up to the observation level. It was frustrating everybody.

"Chillax Weege!" she snapped.

The flickering screens and shaking walls seemed to pitch from the winds, rain and thunder outside. She banged her mouse on the counter and decided to take a walk and look over the rail. There was nothing, just annoying cartoons and plastic toys. She wanted to cry, but tried to be strong for Henry. She closed her eyes and sobbed, thinking of their first date. Someone tugged at her arm.

"Let go Rudy, now's not the time," she said, jerking her arm away. The cold grip held her fast as she turned to face him.

"What the He—AAAAAH!"

Louie held her wrist with an iron grip that she couldn't tear free. Louie was a bearish boy, slightly fish-eyed, round faced and a mouth full of cracked gray teeth.

"Numma! Numma!"

Her legs sagged beneath her, others were screaming as well. She screamed again, ringing her own eardrums at the creepy sight of him.

The boy had nipped her finger, let go and began to trot off in a funny way, holding his ears and cringing. Rudy chased after the boy with an umbrella, roaring like a neutered lion. The closer Rudy got, the more Louie slowed down. The boy turned back towards him, still backing away.

"Numma! Numma!"

The boy backed over a ladder hole and fell down through.

Tori was still screaming in the background.

"It scratched me! It bit me!"

Rudy slammed a lid down over the ladder hole, and latched it shut.

"It can climb. That damn thing can climb! Weege I'll lock the lids—you get her to the medical bay—now!"

She was bawling as she looked at the bloody gash that tore the skin on her hand. There was a deep bite mark on her index finger, dripping blood.

"I don't want to be a zombie!"

Her tiny friend was pulling her along, and she felt helpless in his grasp. Weege shoved her into a white room, along the back wall, that looked like a dentist office with an over-sized circular saw.

"No, no, no Weege! I can't do it!"

"Take off your lab coat!" Weege yelled like an angry cartoon character.

She clutched at it, shaking her head.

"Now woman—or you will be a zombie!" he said in an urgent accent. "Now dammit!"

She did it, and as soon as it fell to the

floor he tied a knot of medical tubing above her bicep. She couldn't believe what was happening, her hand turned cold and numb. She couldn't help but cry. Her hand was pasty and white, lifeless as fallen leaves, while everything above her wrist began to burn. She saw Weege punch a green button on the circular saw and it whirled into action. She was crying uncontrollably now, thoughts filled with despair and Henry.

"I don't want to lose my arm Weege," she pleaded.

"There is no time for drama, close your eyes and shut up!" he said, putting a rod of wood inside her mouth.

She clamped down, tears and mascara mixing into lines and running down her cheeks. He positioned her arm beneath the spinning blade. She wanted to die, be shot, anything but this.

"I don't want to do this."

"Say your prayers!"

She didn't even notice he covered the exposed appendage with a blanket. He jammed a needle in her shoulder, shooting something that burned like fire inside.

"On three!"

She bit down hard praying. *God, don't let this happen!* She was whimpering, lip trembling.

"One!"

He pulled down on the handle with all his might.

SLICE!

"Aaaagh!" Her head was exploding when she blacked out and slumped into the chair.

She woke up and her arm felt like it was burning. She was strapped to the dentist chair and saw Weege wearing green goggles wielding a blow torch. The stench of burnt hair and skin wafted into her nostrils as she writhed in agonizing pain.

Now her own fury was unleashed as she tried to speak.

"What the fah—"

Another needle plunged into her skin, and as she turned to see Rudy's bushy face, the room turned dark as she passed out again.

Rudy stood there, shaking his head in despair, as Weege finished cauterizing the wound. She lay still on the table, like a discarded whore, makeup smeared and soaked with sweat and blood. Her chest rose up and down as he studied her dismembered arm. The flesh was pink above the cut and the rest of her looked fine. He stroked her wet hair from her eyes. *This must be the hottest one-armed chick ever.*

The surgery was finished, she was alive and well, but he couldn't take any chances. The two men left her strapped in the room and secured the door. Louie was still trying to push his way in through the ladder hatch below.

"Watch this," Rudy said as he stood beside the portal. When he screamed, the zombie boy cringed.

Weege pulled up his goggles.

"Hmmm...I've never seen a zombie do that before. Do you think XT Serum works?"

"I don't know, but we're trapped up here unless help comes."

Weege looked worried.

"What if Tori...you know...starts to become a zombie?"

He shook his head saying, "Then we better get some zombie dew."

The zombie boy's head and his mallet hands were banging underneath the latch, shaking the catwalk. They checked their phone signals and no bars showed. They fidgeted, paced, and sweated while waiting, still looking for Henry.

"Numma! Numma! Numma! Numma!" continued to throb in their ears.

CHAPTER 28

BACK IN THE SECURITY ROOM, Jimmy slung a chair into the wall and kicked the old guard's corpse, screaming aloud. They were all alive inside the zombie' arena. He blinked again and again, and tried to figure out why Louie had not bitten them, or at least torn them to bits.

"They should be zombies by now!"

But they weren't. He saw Henry, still trapped in the corridor, pacing while pulling his thick black hair in clenched fists. Tori was harnessed to a table, now missing an arm and out cold. *Good.* The other pair he hated fumbled at their computer stations, shouting back and forth, while Louie tried to press through the metal hatch onto the catwalk. Jimmy wondered if he could release those doors, but he couldn't. He punched the monitor and screamed again. His knuckles bled and he sucked on them as he thought.

He cradled the black case holding the

serum to his chest. *I just got to leave and get paid.*

"The videos! I need the videos!"

He checked the DVR recorders, but there wasn't anything significant on them. No one had been turned, and no one was dead, but Stan. He couldn't let it all end there when he was so close. He had to see them all come to an end. He couldn't leave them around to steal his glory. He had the serum and the notes. He had them all trapped. One by one he pressed the keys and watched his brother in the corridor.

"Let's see how this treats you Henry? It's dinner time, Louie."

CHAPTER 29

HELPLESSNESS CRUSHED HIS WILL. HENRY heard his girl screaming, and he could only imagine the worst. They were all doomed, trapped inside with a monster boy. He hurt his other shoulder trying knock the door aside. He struck it with the butt of his shotgun, denting the shining surface a dozen times.

"Tori! Tori! Tori!" he yelled, his voice full of agony.

He was hoarse, throat dry and spirit broken. Jimmy had done this; he had no doubt. He had two options: wait for a miracle or head for the office. He went inside the elevator and began to pop the hatch in the ceiling.

He could hear the thunder and the beating rain above his ears. A ladder led to the roof where another pair of elevator doors was closed. He had an idea; he could get outside and try to get help. There was a problem, what if he couldn't get the door opened?

Jimmy would have secured it just the same as the rest. He hopped back down inside the elevator, landing hard on his ankle and rolling to the floor.

"Ow!"

It hurt, but he got up despite the agony. He'd had plenty of ankle sprains before. He tried walking if off. *Circulate the blood. Don't get stiff.* What about Stanley, Tori and the rest? He had to help them, or why had he even come back?

He headed toward the security door and pressed his wet ear on the cold metal. He didn't hear a thing. He took out his security card.

"Why not?"

In a limp motion he pressed it over the pad. The door slid back open. He stood gawking, as a wave of cold air mixed in with his sweaty zombie-proof suit. He looked all around, head turning in all directions. He knew something was out there. He grabbed the shotgun, which was propped up along the wall, and stepped outside. Nothing, not a sound could be heard, except the humorous sounds of the TV and symphony music.

He scanned his card, allowing the door to close back, but he wedged the shotgun lengthwise on the sweep. The doorway remained two feet open. He walked into the room, eyes darting and every step more painful than the one before.

"Henry! Henry!" someone was yelling from above, "He's over there—in the ladder shoot. He's in the ladder shoot!"

He could see Rudy's frantic hands motioning across the catwalks. A meaty figure was scrunched inside the metal ladder tube. He saw its head turn, freezing his blood. The boys nostrils flared, in an urgent move it began climbing down the ladder and falling onto the floor.

It can climb! Panic raced though Henry's body.

No one knew what to do, as if all their thoughts became stuck in a snow bank. Someone's mind thawed in time as Louie began coming his way.

"Get up a ladder chute!" It was Weege's shrill voice shouting.

There were several ladder chutes along the walls; he bolted for the closest one. Rudy was running over the top trying to guess where he was going. The boy was coming his way in a stiff trot, elbows locked, and mouth clutching. It sent a jolt of adrenaline through his body. He was faster, running at full speed, oblivious to his swollen ankle, and trying to distance himself further from the boy. He leapt over a set of massive toy blocks that the boy crashed through. *It's fast! Shit! It doesn't look fast!*

Running every direction he could, he created little comfort space. He needed more time to get in the tube. He was exhausted and in a heavy sweat-soaked suit. It occurred to him too late that the suit was slowing him down. *Crap!* He circled around the edges of the room, but every time he got too far away the boy would cut across the middle. His lungs were burning and he was slowing down. He had to go for it. He made another half lap, dashed below one of the tubes and began climbing up. He made it up the first few rungs when his gloved hands slipped, he began to fall, but his foot caught on a rung. Pain lanced through his ankle. Looking down, he saw Louie's clutching mouth and green eyes peering hungrily up his way. Rudy and Weege were screaming for him to move.

Fighting his way up the rungs, he hit the top and pounded away at the locked hatch.

"Open up! Open up! I'm trapped in here!"

He had never felt fear like this. Louie fumbled on the rungs below, lips and jaws smacking, eager to have a bite of him. Henry wasn't sure the suit would stop him from being torn to pieces if Louie got to him. The snap of the latch resounded from above, and the hatch was pulled open with Rudy looking at him eye to eye.

"It's about—*urk*!"

Something powerful was pulling Henry

down. His arm got caught in the rungs, pinching him underneath his armpit. Rudy was trying to pull him up, his bearded face filled with red cheeks and wrought with panic. He could feel the boy's hands crushing his ankle in a mighty grip, something clamped down on his toe like a bear trap. He screamed in agony, drawing a high pitched frightened pig squeal from his friend above. The child's grip and jaws released his toe as Louie fell hard onto the matted floor. Henry didn't look down; he was out of the chute and on the catwalk. Rudy slammed down the door and latched it shut.

He mustered quick breaths as he struggled to pull off his suit.

"Get it off me! I've got to see!"

Rudy stood there, beet-faced, with snot running down his nose. Henry thought he was choking. Rudy pulled out an inhaler and sucked in some white misty air. Now Weege was at his side, helping him jerk off the suit. Henry pulled off his socks and checked his foot and ankles. There were red impressions on his ankle and his toes were bruised, maybe broken, but the skin didn't break.

"Whew!" he said, while looking around, "Where's Tori!?"

CHAPTER 30

A S JIMMY SAT THERE HE couldn't believe they were all okay, after all of his planning. He guzzled another beer as he watched all of them escape a certain death. He knew he had them trapped, but for how long. He needed to leave. He prepared another line of cocaine. Another idea was certain to blossom; they always did. The sight of his brother's face made him angrier by the second. The rest of the crew, trapped inside, were just as bad, always plotting, scheming and wanting to take away his glory.

His words were almost incoherent.

"You shall not have it."

He could see them trying to figure a way out, pointing and thinking out loud. The little man from India's face was a knot of concern, while the fat guy looked like his brain was starving for ice cream. Henry pranced back and forth, the calm inside the storm, pulling them all together to plot against him. He would not let that happen.

He took a heavy snort.

"The glory shall be mine."

He rubbed his reddened nose, noticing a trickle of blood coming down over his lips. "Hate it when that happens."

Taking a handkerchief from his jeans pocket he placed it over his nose and leaned his head back. He needed a plan, a decision... he just had to relax. His mind was a jumbled mess; the clarity he needed to find a direction and make a choice was hard to come by.

He imagined them escaping the facility, being on the news and taking his spotlight. He would be locked up, behind bars, and his brother would be branded the next man that saved the world. All he had to do was kill them all, leave, take the serum and footage to his conspirators, and get paid a handsome fee. That wasn't enough; he wanted more, but that was never discussed; it was only what he wanted. He wanted to be the next Nate McDaniel, and that wouldn't happen while his brother lived. Now his strength was returning, and the sweat of alcohol began to seep from his pores like fumes of clean ideas. Opening his bloodshot eyes he watched the men on the screens. His now brilliant mind hatched another devious plan. Another fit of theatrical laughter passed as he prepared for his next move. His voice was dry as ice as he said, "Yee-hah."

CHAPTER 31

"**S**ENTIENT," HE WHISPERED.

Henry brushed his bangs from his glasses as he watched the footage on the monitor. Weege was fidgeting at his side, while Rudy kept pressing his index finger on the screen.

"Stop touching my screen, dammit," Weege said, smacking the hairy knuckled hand. "I hate it when you do that. Why do you do that?"

Rudy became defensive. "Do you think that really matters *now*—whether or not I touch your screen—when a zombie is about to come up here and eat your fragment of a brain?"

"Okay, cut it out you two. We need to plan, not bicker."

They weren't getting anywhere fast. He'd seen Tori strapped and stabilized to a table and it slammed into his soul. She didn't deserve this; no one did. He felt responsible for it all; he always did. Her expression was peaceful as he held her soft face in his hands, apologizing over and over again. He sobbed inside the madness, trying to remember why he had ever gotten into all of this. His girlfriend had one arm, and he supposed if Stanley could still love his undead mother, he could love a one-armed woman. His dad and brother were another concern. He had no idea where they might be. There was no doubt that Jimmy had caused all of this. And small surprise, either..

He looked again at Nate McDaniel's text. CPWWSZH. *WHS...World Humanitarian Society? Z...Zombie?* He remembered a link Nate had texted moons ago. He scrolled back and opened it up. He broke out in a cold sweat.

"Can't be," he murmured.

He had skimmed the article. He always did that much, but he had neglected to give it any serious thought. Now, with the death of his friend, things seemed to be more... realistic. Inside the article were the other three letters, WPC. *It can't be can it? WPC...World Population Control.* It would explain why China was one of the first nations to fall. Nate had prevented it from going much further. *Wow!* Henry chose to keep that information to himself and move on.

The cracking thunder, driving rain and howling winds did little to cover the sound of Louie hammering at the hatch and moaning, "Numma! Numma! Numma!"

The boy's voice and pounding fists became

stronger by the minute. At any moment he was certain the boy would burst through and life would end.

The facility had been poorly designed, without considering the needs of the staff. They had to rely on cell phones and an old intercom phone system to communicate between the various offices. A fifty-year-old government building had modern technology jammed inside and nothing ever worked the way it should have. Getting people inside to fix it was nearly impossible, and for the most part, out of the question. They were supposed to add an elevator and a fire escape leading to the top observation room, but the funding ran out first. They were supposed to do lots of things, but it never happened. The facility wasn't designed to be a secret lab that housed zombies. They were forced to make do with what they had.

The phone rang and rang on the other end every time he tried to contact Stanley in the lab. His step dad almost never answered the phone, though. He said he never heard it; his mind was always busy. Deep inside, Henry felt something wrong had happened below, but he held out hope.

The failure of both cell phone and land line service squashed the chance of anyone coming to help them, and possible flooding at the bottom of the hills would make things worse if anyone did come. No, they were forgotten for the time being, meant only to fend for themselves. He looked up at the windows, high like an old church, shaking like a tuning fork. On a good day the windows bathed the room in welcome sunlight, but now they were dark and filled with flashes of lightning, some too close for comfort. *Those better hold.*

"Guys, we have to get out of here, I have a plan," Henry said as they gathered around.

"Well, what is it? "Rudy asked.

"We need to trap Louie, like the others. We'll use the dog snares."

The little man objected, hands flailing in the air saying, "We need to kill him and get the hell out of here! How is a doggy thing going to help?"

Rudy rolled his eyes.

"See those poles over there?" Henry pointed at the wall on the other side, "they are what dog catchers use for rabid dogs. They have a noose you flip over the neck to snare them. It's real easy."

Rudy was shaking his bushy head saying, "Henry, he's awful strong. I don't think we can hold him. He about busted that hatch off the hinges. We should try to kill him, it's the only way."

Henry wanted that more than anything, the truth be told, but deep inside he felt killing a child, even though it was undead, was wrong. Now that Louie had just shown them a radical transformation in behavior, the death of another zombie child was even harder to justify. If sound scared Louie, could he feel pain, too? The scientist inside him had to find out. He had to know. Was Stanley that close to curing the zombies, or was this something else?

"No, we can't kill him. Not now. He's just a zombie, we can outsmart him. Rudy, suit up, were going down."

His friend's chin dropped into his chest with a heavy sigh.

Little Weege grabbed him by his lab coat.

"I have an idea! Maybe we just need more zombie dew?"

They all looked at each other, Rudy's eyes holding the most interest, staring at him for the chance.

"Hmmm," Henry said, rubbing his chin. "Maybe he hasn't been fed, maybe Jimmy starved him. Do we have any?"

Rudy's voice was flat.

"It's all downstairs."

They all looked down over the rail as if it were an abyss. Rudy snapped his fingers.

"Wait a minute," he said, running over to Ralph's station. He picked up his red 64-ounce Big Chug cup and said, "It's still got over half a tank. Maybe more..." He shook another half dozen empty cups sitting on the desk. "Nope, these are all gone."

Henry took the 64-ounce cup and folded its waxy top closed. Standing by the rail of the catwalk, he leaned over the ladder chute, eyeing the floor twenty feet below. The catwalk was shaking beneath his feet as Louie pounded away. He held the cup over the rail as his friends tried to guide his aim.

"A little further," Rudy said.

"Back to the left," said Weege.

"No—up to the right."

He glared at them, took simple aim, and dropped it.

Plop!

The cup landed flush on its bottom and they could see liquid splashing up and out, dripping down the cup's side. The top had flipped open, but it was still upright.

"Great shot Bawk!" Rudy said.

Now they waited, and the pounding still came, second after second, minute after... it stopped. Something was climbing back down the ladder and they saw Louie fall to the ground with a thud. The boy was on his knees, sniffing the air.

"Wow, he's sniffing." Henry felt an odd sense of delight.

The boy began licking the drops off the colorful mat, and he snatched up the cup. Louie opened his mouth, wide like a bass fish, bringing a gasp from his audience, then stuffed the cup inside and chomped down with a squish. Henry could hear his heart thumping inside his chest. They all shouted as Louie began walking around; a good bit slower than before, his hunger apparently satisfied.

"Yeah Louie!" Rudy said.

"Don't get too excited. We don't know how long this will last," Henry said. "Wake up Tori. We have to get out of here. I'm going for more dew," he said.

"I'm going too," he felt a delicate hand on his shoulder. It was Weege.

"Thanks Weege, but I've seen you run," he patted the man on the head, "a one-legged zombie could catch you."

Rudy piped in.

"If a clam could run, then that's what it looks like when you run." They all let out an awkward laugh, but the room felt empty.

"Watch my back," he said, heading across the catwalks. As he opened another hatch, his heart raced. He was almost to the bottom when he realized he had forgotten his zombie-proof suit. *Crap!* He moved faster, dropping down like a cat, forgetting his swollen ankle and busted toes, falling to the floor.

"Ow!" he cried, momentarily forgetting where he was.

He staggered up, turning around. He didn't

see or hear the zombie boy. He crept toward the storage room, opened the door and headed inside. He grabbed a few bottles of the zombie dew from the shelves and twisted off a few caps. He grabbed a small bowl. *I've just got to lure him into a cell and we can get out of here.*

"Piece of cake," he said.

As he turned to leave, there was the barrel of a shotgun, pointed in his face.

"Not so fast...Brother."

Jimmy wore a full anti-zombie suit and had a shaking gun in his hands.

"So Henry, you think you figured a way out. I don't think so. Drop the dew!"

Henry could smell rotten teeth and alcohol coming from the face of the mesh mask. He almost gagged. His cranked up brother was up to something he couldn't begin to imagine. He set down the drinks and held his palms up, praying his fool of a brother wouldn't pull the trigger. The shotgun was different from the one he left behind, jamming the door. Jimmy had come prepared.

He tried to sound calm, "What's going on Jimmy? Why are you doing this?"

"Shut up!"

He saw his friends looking down at him in horror, and he saw Louie coming his way. His brother seemed uncertain and tore off his mask, getting a better look around. Louie had moved on. He looked at his brother's distorted face; dried blood covered the edges of his nose and descended down over his puffy lips. Jimmy's head was greasy and flaked, and his pupils were like black marbles.

"I'll do the talking Brother! Tell your stooges to come down here, or I'll blow a hole in you!" Jimmy lowered the weapon on his gut.

"Jimmy, listen to me. Louie might attack any minute. We have to leave. Where is Dad?"

His brothers eyes lit up, his face full of panic and regret. Henry knew at that moment Stanley was dead. It made him angry, angrier than he had ever been.

"Ole Stan was shot! It was an accident! Mom did it!" Confusion seemed to mix with fear in Jimmy's eyes, but they regained their wicked intent.

"Stan's serum is mine! I'll be saving the world, just like Nate McDaniel, and you won't stop me!" His shrill voice resounded from the hard walls of the room. It caught everyone's attention, including the creepy boy who was coming their way.

"Watch out Jimmy!"

His brother turned just in time to see the boy clutching at his back.

KA-BOOM!

It sounded like a cannon went off inside of the facility. As it blasted into the floor, Louie ran, wailing like a frightened swine. Henry leapt onto his brother's back and drove him to the floor. Without even realizing it, he had his hands around his brother's neck, squeezing his eyes from the sockets. His brother couldn't muster a sound as his tongue strained from his mouth. The word *please*, seemed to escape from Jimmy's lips, as reason somehow overcame Henry's animal instinct to kill. He pulled back his arm and punched his brother in the face with a powerful smack, stinging his hand. He did it a few more times and Jimmy lay out cold.

Henry had forgotten everything at that moment. He fought to regain his breath. Someone was screaming and someone else was approaching. He dived for the shotgun, whirled around and blasted it in the air. The boy crouched down, moaning like a frightened animal, and then came his way again, nightmarish and unyielding. Henry remembered Louie tearing apart the rubber ball. His legs turned numb.

He let another blast go into one of the television screens. The boy didn't crouch this time as he came on, an angry look in his gothic face. *He doesn't like the sound.* He didn't have a choice now, it was him or Louie. The zombie boy crept forward, hands clutching, as Henry lowered the barrel at the boy's face. *Sorry Louie.* He pulled the trigger. *Click! — Crap!* He threw the gun at the boy and ran for the drinks. Louie picked up the gun and beat it on the ground, bending the barrel. Henry saw the bottles on the floor, he could hear voices from above telling him to run and he dared not look back. He jumped over his prone brother, tripped over something and fell flat as a stone. Someone had his leg. *Louie!* He turned back and saw his brother's pummeled face.

He kicked away, stretching for a bottle of the juice. An open bottle was just inches from his grasp. He looked back and saw Louie coming back their way.

"Jimmy let go! He's coming!"

His brother looked back, still determined to hold him fast. "I've got a suit, you don't Brother. He's gonna eat your brains—not mine!"

There was no time. Henry drew his leg back and kicked Jimmy hard in the nose with a loud crack. He was free, low crawling back for the bottle, grabbing it in his hand. He tossed it like a grenade into the charging boy's path. A lanky hand snatched the bottle from the air, his brother's beady red eyes intent to reverse his plan. He watched as his brother drew his arm back, liquid sloshing on his suit. Louie crashed into him with his full weight. The drink spilled all over both of them as they thrashed over the bottle.

"Get off me! Get off me!"

Jimmy screamed and kicked, fighting to

free himself from the zombie. The struggle was violent and fast. Henry didn't know what to do. Jimmy faded under the boy's power, trying to crawl away. Louie now clutched the bottle, stuffing it in his throat, sucking the liquid deep inside his belly.

"No! NOOO!" Jimmy screamed, holding a bloody gash where his ear had been bitten off.

Jimmy ran wailing, out of the room and through the security door. Louie was walking listlessly around the room, ignoring several open bottles on the floor. Henry's friends were staring at him in awe from above. Tori stood on weakened legs supported by his friends.

"Come on, we've got to go!" he said, waving for them to come down.

CHAPTER 32

J IMMY'S BLOOD WAS TURNING COLD, but sweeping through him like a fever, and his vision became obscured. Clutching the gash where his ear had been, he screamed all the way down the corridor and ducked into the security room.

The monitors were blurry as he tried to locate his brother. He wanted to shut them back inside, just like before. His fingers were numb and he couldn't find the keys as he slammed down the keyboard. He grabbed the briefcase, felt for the latches and tore them open. He had the syringe in hand and jabbed it into one of the corks of the XT Serum. Drawing out every drop he could, he jammed the long needle deep into his neck and plunged the fluid in, screaming in agony. He fell down, crushing the flask.

His heart pounded with a rush of adrenaline as he lay on the floor, in agony. His veins from head to toe were streams of electricity. He lay still one long moment. His vision began to return, but his limbs became stiff and strong. Rising from the floor, he groaned and shoved everything he needed in the case and latched it. He saw a glimpse of himself reflecting off the stainless steel walls. He was tall and rangy, with a busted nose, bloody chin and rising blue veins. He licked his lips and rubbed his face. If this is what being undead felt like, it felt pretty good. It felt great. But how long would it last? He would worry about that later.

He headed toward the back security door on legs of steel. He scanned his card and went out into the driving rain. He couldn't feel the wind or hail tearing into his face. A tree had fallen nearby, crushing the chain link fence before him. He could see a swarm of black vehicles blocked by another tree in the distance. Armed men in black were swarming out and heading inside. He had to run and hide. Or did he? He hid in the darkness of the storm as they all passed by. A lone man stood outside in the rain, watching the vehicles, somehow smoking a cigarette. Jimmy fought the urge to eat the man whole as he snuck behind him.

The man turned on him, shotgun level at his head. He was small, wearing dark sunglasses, with a black moustache and jutting lower lip. The man's southern voice was deep as a river.

"Whatcha doin' Zombie?"

"I'm not a zombie! I'm a man...Jimmy!" he shouted.

"You sure look like a zombie!"

Something sounded familiar about the man. The voice on the phone—his contact? Was that him? He recalled something.

"I'm Jimmy Bawkula. JB 111."

The man gave him a curious look and lowered his gun.

"Is that the XT Serum in the case Jimmy?"

Jimmy thought he was smiling when he said it.

"Everything you asked for."

The man shouldered his shotgun and held out his hands. He handed over the case and watched the man open it. The notes, videos and vials were all there.

"Where's the other flask? Weren't there two?"

"The other one is in me. I got bitten," he pointed at his bloody earhole, "so I injected myself."

The man closed the brief case.

"Is that so? How do you feel?"

"Like a million dollars! The serum works!"

He knew he was smiling. His reward was on the way.

"That's good to know. Fascinating...my boss will love that."

"Great!"

The small man had a half-smile, half-sneer on his face and his voice changed to ice water.

"Well Jimmy...you don't look like a million dollars."

He managed to laugh and shrug.

"Well, I guess I don't."

"No Boy...you look like a zombie."

Jimmy watched in slow motion as the man procured a semi-automatic pistol from thin air and pointed it at his head. He saw the fires of Hell when it exploded in his face.

EPILOGUE

I̤T WAS A SPECIAL NIGHT at the campfire as people of all ages were gathered around an older man with an excited face and graying beard. Fathers, sons, mothers, daughters and cousins shared hotdogs, s'mores, hot cocoa and beer, as the owls hooted and the tree frogs croaked. Everyone at the campsite was hanging on the man's every word. His deep, melodious voice had drawn in all ears over the span of the past few hours. He rubbed his calloused hands together as he continued, while another man dropped another log on the blazing fire.

"When Henry, Tori, Rudy and Weege finally made it out of the facility, the skies began to clear. The men in the black cars said they were with the World Humanitarian Society and they took over the place. Henry tried to tell them what was going on inside with the children, but they didn't seem to listen. But, Henry never told them about the message

Nate McDaniel sent. He was afraid they might kill him right then and there...but it didn't happen. It was a sad day when he buried Stanley and his mother Linda. He had been given the authority to euthanize her, and he slept better after that."

"What happened to Tori," a teenage girl with curly auburn hair urged.

"Tori turned out just fine and got her old job back at Fast-Mart."

There was an awkward silence.

"I'm kidding," he said, patting her on the knee. "She and Henry got married not long after that, and he took a job as a school teacher and basketball coach. She stayed home baking cookies and making babies. They had a happier life."

"What about Rudy and Weege?" a boy, about eight, asked.

"Well, they both moved to Las Vegas and became casino dealers."

"That doesn't make any sense," someone said.

"Hey—what about the zombie kids, what happened to all of them?"

The old story teller didn't say anything at first as he stirred a stick in the ground.

"As far as anyone knew, the WHS took them somewhere else. All but the one they couldn't find...Louie."

Someone gasped as another young voice

said, "You mean he's still out there Grandpa?" There were uncertain looks and a few cracked smiles on the shadowy faces of the rest of the folks.

"No Boy, he ain't out there...He's right behind you! Run!"

Half of the camp jumped, while the rest fell over in laughter as the children screamed, scrambling to their parents. Heavy laughs came here and there until they all subsided. Some of the children were crying. The older ones were laughing. One boy, about twelve years old, was lying near the fire, looking up at the dark and distant hilltop called Guthrie. His name was Fergie, and he hated that story, but only because he knew it was true. Things had never been the same in the world since the day he and his grandpa raced away from the facility, home of the Zombie Day Care.

NOTE FROM THE AUTHOR

I wanted to address a few things about the story. It's a short novel, just over 37,000 words. I love writing short stories and I have dozens more that I plan to release, old and new. Zombie Day Care is a ridiculous idea (zombies slowed down by sugary caffeinated drinks, unlike the living) come to life. I wanted to try my own spin on the zombies as well. What happens when people get them under control? How does the world react? What do we do with them? I'll fill in more details about who is behind the zombie outbreak in the second book, Zombie Rehab. The 3rd book, Zombie Warfare will be released early 2014.

I don't know if this series will go beyond 3 books, but I'm not ruling it out. My main genre is fantasy. But if you like the others Zombie Impact books we'll see.

Thanks for reading and if you have time an honest review would be nice.

Don't stop,

Craig Halloran

ABOUT THE AUTHOR

Craig Halloran is a veteran, husband and father. He enjoys sports (mostly football), working out, fishing, writing, watching TV and entertaining mankind. His books are filled with endless action, exciting characters and compelling stories. He resides with his family outside of his hometown of Charleston, West Virginia. When he isn't writing stories he is seeking adventure, working out, or watching sports. To learn more about him go to: www.thedarkslayer.com

OTHER WORKS BY
CRAIG HALLORAN

The Darkslayer: Wrath of
the Royals (Book 1)
The Darkslayer: Blades in the Night (Book 2)
The Darkslayer: Underling Revenge (Book 3)
The Darkslayer: Danger and
the Druid (Book 4)
The Darkslayer: Outrage in
the Outlands (Book 5)
The Darkslayer: Chaos at
the Castle (Book 6)

The Chronicles of Dragon: The Hero, The
Sword and the Dragons (Book 1 of 10)

Zombie Day Care - Impact Series: Book 1
Zombie Rehab - Impact Series: Book 2
Zombie Warfare - Impact Series: Book 3

It's Not Him; It's them

Connect with him at:
Facebook: The Darkslayer Report by Craig
Twitter: Craig Halloran

Printed in Great Britain
by Amazon